Cottonwood

GAYLORD M

SHADOW
OF THE
GALLOWS

SHADOW OF THE GALLOWS

•

S. J. Stewart

AVALON BOOKS
NEW YORK

PRINTED IN THE UNITED STATES OF AMERICA
ON ACID-FREE PAPER
BY HADDON CRAFTSMEN, BLOOMSBURG, PENNSYLVANIA

To my sons Randy and Richard,
who have added so much to my life.

Chapter One

Dan Newland stopped to look back over the trail and give the dun a breather. Heat waves rose from the desert floor beneath a sky empty of clouds. There was no sign of the man who was following him, but he was back there, somewhere, and Draper wasn't his only enemy. This land was the domain of the Apache. Dan rode on with caution.

After a time, he stopped again. It was wise to conserve the big horse's strength, for he would have to rely on that strength to survive. Dan wiped a sleeve across his face, and it came away with a film of dust mixed with sweat. He took a swig from his canteen, letting the tepid water wash his mouth and run down his throat. There was a temptation to drink more. He resisted it, and after a brief rest he urged the dun forward. A prudent man didn't linger long, nor flaunt his whereabouts in this part of Arizona Territory. Dan was twenty-six and far from a greenhorn. He'd learned the tricks of survival years ago at his father's side.

He kept out of sight as best he could, circling

around the rises rather than topping them. Once he followed a narrow wash for miles. The way he chose was longer and more difficult, but it was safer. His butternut shirt and pants blended well with the desert background.

Shadows were lengthening when he came around a low hill and spotted the wagon. It was just setting there among the big cactuses, alone and vulnerable to attack. Two mules were hitched to the buckboard, and two horses were fastened behind. Dan reined up and looked the situation over. An old man with stooped shoulders stood close to the mules. His rifle was in his hand. His only companion was a boy who was still a few years from being a man. Dan tried to imagine what had brought them to this dangerous place.

It was the boy who caught sight of him first. The kid touched the old man's sleeve in warning, causing him to straighten and look in Dan's direction.

"Hello the wagon," Dan called belatedly.

"Come on in if you be friendly" was the answer.

Dan rode toward them slowly, in what he hoped was an unthreatening manner. He noticed that the kid's hand was never far from the revolver at his side. The boy wasn't a trusting soul, and that was good. The ones who trusted strangers often ended up dead. Dan was aware that his appearance did little to inspire confidence. His features were angular, and any softness about them had been worn away, long ago, by life's hard lessons. He had no extra flesh on his body, and his dark brown beard was covered with dust. The clothes that he wore were far from new, and they were as dusty as his beard.

"Light and rest a spell, son," invited the old man. "What is it that brings you way out here to the middle of nowhere?"

Dan felt irritation at the intrusive question. He dismounted before he answered.

"I could ask you the same thing, but I won't. As for me, I'm looking for a place to settle down and stay awhile. Figured on lookin' over the high country farther north. Maybe start my own ranch."

The lie had come so easily that it astonished him. In fact, to his own ears it had sounded like the truth.

"You got yourself a good plan," said the man as he stuck out his hand. "The name's Asher Quigley. Ash to my friends. Standin' over there with the glum face is Tony."

Dan shook his hand.

"I'm Dan Newland, recently from Texas by way of California."

"Glad to know you."

The kid stayed in the background, wearing a hostile expression.

"Say, if you'd like to work on somebody else's ranch until you get your own place, you're welcome to come to work for the Lazy Q. Me and my brother, Simon, have us a little spread north of here, and we can sure use your help."

Ash's offer brought a choking sound from the kid, and Dan couldn't resist bedeviling him.

"I accept," he said.

The old man beamed.

"Fine, fine. Glad to have you along with us. Now, we'd better get moving before Apaches come along and decide to lift our scalps."

Dan climbed back into the saddle while his new companions got on the buckboard. There was little daylight left as they journeyed across the arid land. Just days ago, Fort Yuma had been buzzing with the news of recent Apache raids. A large band was said to be holed up somewhere in the Mazatzal Mountains, a range that lay to the east. But in fact, they could be anywhere, and they could strike at any time.

"How much farther to your ranch?" Dan asked.

"Oh, four or five days' ride, maybe. That is, if we're lucky."

Luck wasn't something that Dan counted on much, although he figured that each man had his share of good and bad. Mostly, he liked to think that a man made his own luck, and that he dealt with the bad things that came along as best he could.

He had to credit it to good luck, though, that he'd seen Draper bellied up to that bar in Yuma before Draper spotted him. Otherwise, he'd have been forced into yet another gunfight. As it happened, Dan had simply backed out of the bar, collected his things, and left town. It wasn't that he was afraid to face the gunman, at least not any more than usual. It was just that Draper was one more in a chain of gunfighters, drawn by the circumstances of Dan's growing reputation. Unfortunately, if Draper was so determined that he'd followed him from Texas, he would surely follow him across the Arizona desert.

All around him, the landscape was dotted with large saguaro cactuses. A sergeant back at the fort had told him they could weigh a ton or more. In the twilight, they looked to Dan like strange ghosts that were keeping vigil over the vast, hostile desert.

They rode in silence now. He often scanned the distant hills for sign of the Apache. He also watched the trail behind for his other enemy.

After the sun had dipped low beyond the horizon and stars were appearing, they stopped and made camp in a small depression. Ash burrowed into his supplies and passed around jerked beef. The kid shrugged deeper into his coat as a refuge against the night-cold and the remnant of wind that refused to die. He took one reluctant bite of what the old man offered and began to complain in a high-pitched voice.

"Grandpa, why can't we start a fire and cook a hot meal?"

The old man lowered himself to a sitting position and rested his back against the wheel of the buckboard.

"I don't think it'd be smart to advertise our whereabouts. Not to the Indians, and not to whoever it is that's after our friend, here."

Dan had put the last of the piece of jerky in his mouth and was spreading his bedroll a few yards from the wagon. He tensed when he heard Ash's words. The kid didn't waste any time. He marched over and stood directly in front of Dan with his hand on his hip.

"I knew it! You're nothing but a dad-blamed out-law. How dare you join up with us when you're running from a posse."

To Dan, the kid looked like a bantam rooster flopping its wings and clucking at an intruder. He laughed in spite of himself.

"Do you really think anyone could put together a posse to follow me out here into Apache country, no matter what I'd done? I'm one man and no danger to you."

He hoped the part about the danger was true.

The kid backed off a little, thinking it over.

"You're running from somebody, though, aren't you?"

"I reckon that's strictly my own business and none of yours."

This set him off again.

"You've got another thing coming. It is my business and Grandpa's business, too, if somebody is apt to come riding into our camp shooting at us."

Much as he hated to admit it, Dan conceded that young Tony had a point. They were decent folks, and they had a right to know what was going on.

"There's a fellow who wants to put a bullet into me. He followed me from Texas, and I spotted him in Fort Yuma. I left town without him seeing me, but I expect he's on my trail. There were others who saw me leave."

What he said made him sound like a coward, he knew. But he didn't know how else to say it.

"So you're running away," Tony said. "Just what did you do that made this man so anxious to put you six feet under?"

Before he answered, Dan crawled into his bedroll and let his weary muscles relax. The kid was nosy, no two ways about it. But he'd started this so he figured that he might as well finish it.

"I killed his brother in a fair fight, one that he insisted on having. That part doesn't matter to Draper, though. He wants to get even. Blood for blood."

Ash got to his feet and leaned against the wagon.

"We've got a chance of getting to the ranch before this fellow catches up to you," he said. "If he shows up there, we'll send him packing."

Dan was beginning to like the old-timer. But Ash didn't know what kind of man Ben Draper was. He was like a bulldog who had the seat of your britches in his teeth. He aimed to hang on and never let go.

"Why did his brother want to shoot you?" Tony asked with a curiosity that appeared to have no end to it.

"You hush right now, Missy," Ash scolded. "You've asked enough questions. Some things is private, and a man don't want to talk about 'em."

Dan sat up. Had Ash called Tony "Missy"? Maybe he'd heard wrong.

As if a charade had ended, the kid pulled his hat off, letting waist-length hair tumble down. A closer look confirmed that she was a young woman, though it wasn't easy to tell in those baggy men's clothes that she wore. Moonlight glinted off honey-colored strands as she shook her head like a high-spirited filly. He could see well enough to tell that if somebody was to put her into a nice dress she'd be downright beautiful.

"Stop your staring," she ordered. "Don't think that I don't know you're doing it."

He felt his face grow hot, for what she said was true. He was indeed staring, and he scarcely knew how to stop.

"You'll have to overlook Tony's bad manners," Ash apologized. "She ain't been brought up like a proper young lady ought to be."

"Thank heaven for that" was her retort. "I'm not, and never will be, a 'proper young lady.' "

Dan had no doubts about that.

His companions spread their bedding some distance away from his own. The mules and horses were picketed nearby.

"There's no use to post a guard tonight," Ash said. "I sleep with one eye open all the time, and the least little thing that happens wakes me right up."

Dan had his doubts, but he wasn't in any mood to argue with him.

"Fine," he said, wondering how the old man had managed to live so long with his cavalier attitude toward caution. He decided that maybe it would be a good idea to keep one eye open, himself.

He drifted into a light sleep, keeping one part of his mind attuned for any unusual noise. But no danger presented itself to awaken him. They broke camp shortly before sunrise. He noticed that Tony's hair was tucked back under her hat once more. Without a word, she climbed onto the seat of the buckboard next to her grandfather, pretending that Dan didn't exist. That was okay with him. He hadn't had much luck with women, and he had more important things to worry about than this one's rudeness.

In spite of his circumstances, he found himself enjoying another Arizona dawn. The eastern sky was awash in a glow that would soon fade in the glory of the sun. It seemed to him that there was something mystical about the time cycle, and no matter how many beginnings he watched, the birth of a new day would never become ordinary to him.

He shivered in the morning chill. Later, it would be hot even though it was fall, and the mountain peaks to the north were capped in white.

"There's some good folks who don't live far from here," Ash said. "We'll stop at their place for a while and water the animals. Maybe get some coffee for ourselves. Harry and Enid Paxton are always hospitable. You're goin' to like 'em, Dan."

"I'd be pleased to meet your friends," he said.

He noted that the ranches were few in number in this part of the Territory, and mostly they were far apart in distance. The war had caused Washington to pull all of the troops away from Arizona and send them to the Rio Grande Valley. It had been nothing less than abandonment, leaving the civilian population to cope as best it could with marauding bandits and Indians. Some of those troops had been returned, now that the war had been over for years, but they hadn't yet succeeded in ending the raids on isolated ranches. The ranchers who insisted on staying were either foolish or very brave, depending on how you looked at it.

It was almost midday when they neared the Paxton ranch and sighted the burned ruins that had been the couple's home. They rode into the yard and viewed a grim scene. The Paxtons and three of their men had been murdered, and the stock was gone. He saw that Tony's face was pale, and she looked sick. Dan felt sick, himself, and he'd been in the midst of battle during the war. He dismounted and felt the ashes. They were cold.

The way the Paxtons and the others had died was not a pretty sight. It was something that Tony shouldn't have to see. She was staring off in the distance now, as if in some kind of trance. Ash Quigley swore, though he didn't size up to being a swearing man. Dan could understand how he must feel.

"We'd better hurry up and bury them," he urged. "The Apaches may be long gone, but it's best not to count on it."

Ash climbed down from the buckboard and found a shovel among his things. They buried the dead near a spot where Enid Paxton had been nurturing a patch of desert marigolds. When the unpleasant chore was finished, Ash took off his hat and said a few words that Dan recognized as Scripture. Tony stood silently beside him, lost in her own thoughts.

"Let's be on our way," Ash said when he'd finished. "I'm worried about my brother and the others."

Tony gave a start, as if her mind had returned from wherever it had been.

"Grandpa, you don't think they're in danger, do you?"

He put his arm around her shoulders.

"Probably not, granddaughter, but it's best to be prudent."

Dan found himself in agreement. He wondered if the plight of the Paxtons had served as a warning to Ash, for in his opinion, taking Tony into the desert hadn't been prudent at all. Neither was his failure to stand watch at night.

They didn't waste any time taking their leave of the place that would no longer hold good memories for the Quigleys. For his own part, Dan was relieved to put behind him the stench of death.

The miles passed while each of them dealt with his own feelings. Dan wasn't good with words, and he had no idea what he could say that would comfort them. In the end he decided that perhaps grief is better eased in silence.

When it came time to stop for the night, it was Ash who suggested taking turns standing watch.

"I'd feel a whole lot easier," he said.

"Fine," Dan agreed. "I'll take the first one."

He pulled the .44 Winchester rifle from its scabbard and found himself a place some distance beyond the wagon.

"I'll get some sleep and spell you later," Ash promised.

Dan watched as he crawled under the covers. Tony was already bedded down just beyond her grandfather. While they slept, Dan sat watching the night. The silence around him was disturbed only by a few sounds of nature, and Ash's raspy snores, which weren't natural at all.

It worried him that the burial detail, necessary though it had been, had cost so much time. Riding beside the Quigleys' buckboard had slowed him down, as well. He had no doubt that Draper was gaining on him. The danger of armed Apache wouldn't stop the gunman either. He wanted vengeance, and he liked to kill.

The irony was that Dan had tried to avoid trouble that day in the small Texas town. But Sonny Draper was a hotheaded kid out to make a reputation for himself. He wanted to kill the man who'd outdrawn Lawson Tate. But when the smoke cleared, Sonny Draper was the one who lay sprawled in the middle of the dusty street. The circumstances, though, didn't matter to his brother.

The fact remained that Dan had a reputation now. Having shot Tate and one of the Draper brothers, there would be others wanting to test themselves against him. To free himself, he had no choice but to leave and start over in a new place. He hadn't reckoned with his past following him.

Much of the night had passed when Ash crawled out of his bedroll and rubbed the stiffness from his limbs. He picked up his rifle and walked over to where Dan was standing watch.

"Get some sleep," he said. "Tomorrow is apt to be demanding."

Dan was tired, and he had no doubt that the day to come would be demanding. They all were. He'd grown used to it.

He crawled into the warmth of his bedroll, and when sleep came, so did dreams. They were filled with long honey-colored tresses and eyes that were robin's egg blue. But a shadow hovered at the edge of his dreams. It had no recognizable form, only a sense of menace.

He opened his eyes to the grayness just before dawn and saw that it was Tony who was standing guard with Ash's rifle. Ash was building a small fire.

Dan figured it was safe enough. No one would be able to spot it.

For a few minutes, he lay there pretending he was still asleep. But the aroma of coffee reached him, and when Ash put some bacon on to fry, there was a rumbling in his stomach that he couldn't ignore. He got up and pulled his boots on. It seemed that no matter how bad things got, a cup of hot coffee and a plate of food had the power to lift a man's spirits.

"You're just in time for breakfast," Ash said.

The three of them fueled themselves for the day's journey.

"You've probably noticed that I'm anxious to get back to the ranch," Ash said when the grub was nearly gone.

"Believe you mentioned it a time or two," Dan said.

Tony paused, her cup halfway to her lips.

"Don't worry, Grandpa. The Apaches won't attack that far north, and even if they do, Uncle Simon can take care of himself. He has Aaron, Kearney, and the others."

Ash leaned over and patted her on the shoulder.

"I reckon you're right, honey. Just humor an old man, and let's get goin'."

Dan had a hunch that he wanted to get Tony to the relative safety of the ranch a whole lot more than he was worried about the safety of the ones already there. He guessed that Ash was worried about Draper too. Dan couldn't blame him for that. What he couldn't understand was why the old man had made such a dangerous trip with his granddaughter in the first place. There must have been a compelling reason.

They packed away the things, and in record time the mules were hitched, the horses saddled, and they were under way. All the while they'd been heading northeast, they'd been gaining altitude. Trees replaced the saguaro that had been so prevalent before. As the hours passed, the air grew warmer, but not as warm as it had been in the low country. Dan was impressed by the beauty around him.

After a time, Tony left the buckboard and mounted the chestnut mare. It was no surprise to Dan that she rode astraddle like a man. She'd been keeping her distance, so he wasn't expecting it when she rode up beside him.

"It's lovely, isn't it, Dan?" she said, making a sweeping motion with her arm to encompass the visible world around them.

He noticed that, for the first time, she called him by name. He was glad to see her recovering a little from the horrors of the Paxton ranch.

"I'll have to agree with you there," he replied. "Can't say that I've seen a whole lot that could match it."

"All of this beauty makes the struggle to survive worthwhile, doesn't it?"

Above him, the sky was bright blue with wispy clouds here and there. Around him was the vast space of the Territory.

"I can't deny it's a pretty sight, but it's not exactly tame."

"No it isn't. But maybe someday it will be. And

maybe we won't like it as well if there's not any challenges to keep us aware of how precious life is.''

So Tony was the kind of woman who liked challenges. Well, that wasn't a surprise. He just hoped that she wouldn't have to face anything that she and her grandfather couldn't handle.

He traveled with the buckboard for two more days without a sign of Draper. There was no sign of Apache either. It was on the afternoon of the third day that they rode through the front gate of the Lazy Q. They were met by a portly man with a broad face and jowls. He was taller than Ash, and he appeared to be several years younger. Simon Quigley was relieved that his brother and grandniece had arrived safely with their scalps still in place, although he was surprised to see that Tony had returned.

''You've been worrying the daylights out of me,'' he scolded Ash. ''I can't understand why you insisted on taking Tony to Fort Yuma all by yourself.''

''Couldn't spare anyone to go with us. Everybody was needed here. Besides, we had a better chance if we didn't draw attention to ourselves.''

Dan noticed that Simon looked skeptical.

''Well, you're back now,'' he said, ''and that's what's important. Since Tony's with you, I guess things didn't work out like you'd planned.''

''Nope. Expect you'll be hearin' about it later.''

Dan wondered about what hadn't worked out. Tony didn't seem to be too disappointed.

''And who's this?'' Simon asked, turning his attention to Dan.

Dan offered his hand.

''The name's Dan Newland.''

"We run into him in the desert," Ash explained. "Or rather he run into us. I offered him a job, and being the smart fellow that he is, he took it."

Simon grasped his hand with the grip of a grizzly and pumped it up and down.

"Glad to have you with us. Over yonder is the bunkhouse. Go and make yourself at home."

"Much obliged," said Dan, looking at the long, narrow structure Simon had pointed out. He grabbed his gear and headed toward it.

Ash would no doubt fill in the details of the journey for his brother, including what they'd found at the Paxtons'.

He couldn't help noticing that the Quigleys had done a lot of work on their place. With the plentiful supply of trees, the buildings were made of wood rather than the adobe that was used for construction farther south. Here, the air was scented with pine and cedar, a pleasant change from desert dust. The altitude made it refreshingly cool. He liked this part of the country and decided he could get used to it real easy. Then he shrugged off the notion. This was no time to think of settling down, not with a gunman tracking him to kingdom come.

Inside the bunkhouse everything was neat and clean. He walked over and stowed his gear in one corner, after first retrieving a pair of field glasses. Then he went outside again to have a look around. The high ground gave him a vantage point from which to view the whole area to the south. He went past the corral and over to where the landscape sloped steeply downward. Along the edge several cedars grew, giving him a measure of cover as he scanned the countryside with the glasses. At first glance, that part of the world appeared to be empty of humanity. Then he thought he saw something. It looked like a horse and rider, but the image was brief, just long enough to register on his consciousness, and then it was gone.

Tony's footstep betrayed her approach.

"Are you looking for that man who wants to kill you?" she asked as she came up beside him.

"I'm just being cautious," he said.

"Well, did you see anything?"

She was still being nosy, and her persistence annoyed him. Still, he didn't want to give her the satisfaction of knowing this.

"I'm not sure," he answered. "For an instant, I thought I saw a horse and rider, but whoever it was disappeared."

"Here, let me have a look," she said, reaching for the glasses.

He handed them over.

While he watched, she put them to her eyes and peered into the distance.

"I can't see anything that's not supposed to be there. I think you're getting so skittish that you're imagining things."

Annoyance turned to anger. Tony had a certain knack for stirring his emotions. The worst part was how much she seemed to enjoy it.

"Oh, there you are, Tony," came Simon Quigley's booming voice as he approached. "I wondered where you'd gone off to."

He noticed the field glasses in her hand.

"Is something wrong?" he asked.

"No. Nothing's wrong," Tony said. "It's just that our new hired hand is a little nervous about one of his old friends, that's all. His fear is making him see things that aren't there."

Dan clenched his teeth to keep from saying something he'd regret. His hands clenched as well. If Simon sensed the tension, he pretended to ignore it.

"Let me have a look," he said.

Tony handed the glasses over to her uncle, and he too scanned the horizon.

"Don't see a thing," he conceded. "But that don't mean he's not out there. You could hide a herd betwixt here and yonder."

Dan agreed. The terrain was rugged, with plenty of places to keep out of sight.

"Draper is bound to show up sooner or later," he said. "It's best to see him first, before he gets here."

Simon didn't seem unduly worried.

"Trouble is something we're used to in these parts. Seems like it's got to come around and check on us from time to time to keep us on our toes."

He handed the field glasses back. Tony realized that she wasn't the center of attention the way she usually was, so she took off her hat and let her hair fall free, as he'd seen it that first night on the desert. He wished that she'd leave it that way.

"I still think you're imagining things," she announced. "A man would have to be downright crazy to ride across the desert with the Apaches stirred up the way they are."

"Crazy like your grandfather, and like myself," he couldn't resist saying.

That didn't set well with her. Without another

word, she turned and flounced back to the house. At least she flounced as much as she could in the over-size pair of man's worn-out britches that she wore.

Dan figured that she was wrong about Draper. He might not want to be seen just yet, but the gunman was out there somewhere. Dan could feel it in his bones.

Chapter Two

Simon just stood there for a minute looking puzzled by his niece's reaction. Then he shrugged and turned to Dan.

"Ash is fixin' supper. He's a pretty good cook, although I wouldn't mention it to him. It might go to his head. Anyway, we're expecting you to come to the house and eat with us."

"I'll be there," Dan said.

He hoped that Tony's mood would improve by suppertime, for he'd welcome a good meal for a change.

They parted company, with Simon heading toward the house and Dan going back to the bunkhouse. He wanted to make himself more presentable. Against one wall there was a stand with a chipped pitcher and bowl setting on it. He filled the pitcher with well water and poured it into the bowl. It felt good to dip his hands and splash the cool water onto his face. When that was done, he washed his thick mop of hair and smoothed it down. A glance into the cracked piece of mirror above the stand showed him the reflection of a man who looked almost civilized, if not handsome. He pulled a clean shirt from his saddlebags. As he put it on, he thought about how little it took to make a man feel like a human being. Now he reckoned that all he needed was a good meal and a night of uninterrupted sleep.

He was halfway to the house when he smelled the aroma of fresh coffee drifting on the air. There were other good smells coming his way too. It appeared that Simon had been right about his brother's cooking skills.

It was Simon who let him in when he knocked on the door. Dan glanced around the Quigleys' sturdy cabin. It was larger than most of the ones he'd seen in this part of the country. A stone fireplace took up the biggest part of one end of it. On the mantle, a round-face clock ticked the seconds loudly. Two bunks were stacked against one of the long walls, and a table stood in the middle of the room. It was the kind that could be folded and put away when not in use. He couldn't see the other end of the cabin. It was curtained off with green flowered calico, most likely to make a private sleeping area for Tony.

"Sit down here at the table, Dan, and make yourself at home," Ash invited before he turned back to his work at the fireplace.

Simon seated himself on a stool in one corner and resumed whittling on a knickknack of some sort.

Tony had briefly acknowledged him when he first arrived, but said nothing else. Now, she took down some plates from a shelf and began to set the table. He watched her deft movements and noticed her graceful hands.

"There's just going to be the four of us this evening." Ash said. "The rest of the boys are gone."

"We're awfully short on men as you can see," Simon said. "And the ones we have are busy right now. We've got so many head of cattle missing that I sent them out to look for strays."

Ash snorted at his brother's comment. Without a word, he leaned over and set a biscuit-filled platter on the table beside the other bowls. Then he seated himself across from Dan. Tony and Simon joined them.

"Help yourself," his new boss invited.

Dan took him up on the invitation and heaped his plate with beans, biscuits, and greens.

"Grandpa thinks that cattle rustlers are operating in this area," Tony said. "With all the losses we've suffered, I think so too."

"Well, it wouldn't be the first time something like that has happened," Dan said. "Have any of your neighbors come into sudden prosperity?"

The question made Simon look uncomfortable.

"I wouldn't want to make any accusations," he said, "for that could cause a whole lot of trouble, and I might be wrong."

"Well, it don't trouble me none to make an accusation," Ash said. "There's a fellow who's got himself a spread west of here, and he's hired a bunch of riffraff to work for him. He goes by the name of Noah Keaton, and he's doin' real well by all appearances. A little too well, in fact, for a man who's only been here a short time, and who started with next to nothing."

"He's not a bit friendly either," Tony said. "His

men nearly killed Aaron Locke, awhile back, when they caught him trying to get a look at the brand on one of their steers to see if it wasn't one of ours.''

''Sounds suspicious,'' Dan said between bites.

''It made me plumb mad,'' Ash said. ''Why, that boy wasn't full growed when he started working for us. I'd hate to see anything bad happen to him.''

Tony got a worried look on her face.

''You don't suppose Aaron would be foolhardy enough to go back and snoop around on his own, do you?''

''Of course not,'' her uncle reassured her. ''The boy's a little headstrong, but he wouldn't take a risk like that again. Besides, the others are with him, and Kearney O'Malley is one sensible Irishman.''

Dan didn't speak his mind, but he was thinking that if you wanted to find something that was missing, you'd go and look in the place where it was apt to be. What was the use otherwise? It seemed to him that Aaron was the cowboy with the common sense. It sounded like he had some starch in his backbone too.

Dan was enjoying the meal. The hot food was filling the emptiness in his stomach, and he rather liked sitting across from Tony too, even though she was unusually quiet.

''Now that I'm working for the Lazy Q,'' he said, ''it might be a good idea for me to ride out in the morning and see if I can help.''

Ash looked pleased at his suggestion. ''Good idea. But morning comes early around here, same as it does other places. If you've had your fill of grub,

I'll walk you out to the bunkhouse. I need to exercise these old legs of mine.''

Dan suspected that Ash was a lot more eager to exercise his jaw than his legs. Most likely he had something to say that he didn't want the others to hear. Dan drained his cup and stood up.

"That was a fine meal," he complimented "Now, I'll say good night."

"Good night," Simon echoed, while Tony merely nodded.

Dan stepped outside into the frosty air. The moon was shining like a big opal in the clear night sky. Breezes gentled their way through millions of pine needles, playing a lullaby that pleasured his ears. Ash walked beside him.

"Dan, I know that you've got troubles of your own without taking on any of ours," he said, "but things got worse around here while I was gone to Yuma. We can't afford to keep on losing cattle like we've been doing. Simon's not the one to be in charge, either. He just ain't got the right temperament for taking care of rustlers."

From what Dan had learned of Simon Quigley, he had to agree. The two brothers were as different as silk and sandpaper.

"Aaron and the others are good men," Ash went on, "but they need the right kind of leader. I'd take on the job, myself, but the years have been weighing me down of late. I ain't as spry as I used to be."

Dan was struck by the irony of the situation. He'd left Texas and come all this way to get rid of trouble. But not only had trouble followed him in the person of Ben Draper, more of it had entangled him through Ash and Tony Quigley.

They reached the bunkhouse door, and he stopped and turned to the older man.

"You hired me on, so I'll do whatever it is that needs to be done."

The old man sighed as if a weight had been taken off his shoulders.

"I knew I could count on you, son. You're a man that'll go the distance."

Dan watched him amble back to the lamp-lit cabin. Then he let himself into the deserted bunkhouse, where he bedded down for the night. When he closed his eyes, Ash's last words kept running through his mind. Had he ever truly gone the distance? It always seemed to him that it was smarter to leave a place, and to avoid confrontation, than to seek it out, or simply allow it to happen. He'd had two senseless confrontations in spite of his reluctance to do so. They were more than plenty. Now, he wanted a new kind of life, one that was free from his reputation. It was becoming clear that he wasn't going to get it without a fight.

The following morning, just as Dan climbed out of bed, Ash was at the door with breakfast.

"I was fixin' my own," he said, "and thought I might as well cook enough for two. The others are still asleep. Simon never was much for getting up with the sun, and Tony was plumb wore out after that trip."

He came in and handed Dan a full plate. Then he set the coffeepot down beside the bowl and pitcher.

Next, he fetched a couple of enameled cups from a
narrow shelf and filled them from the pot.

Simon kept chickens, and the plate was heaped
with scrambled eggs and bacon. Dan couldn't remember the last time that he'd eaten a fresh egg. He
dug in with an appetite.

Ash sat on a bunk across from him and drank his
coffee slowly. Dan figured he had something on his
mind that he wanted to talk about. He was right.

"Dan, my brother told me that Aaron was supposed to check in today. When he gets here, I want
you to go back with him to meet the others. I'm
going to tell him that you've been hired as the new
foreman who's going to fill the opening that Lom-
bard left."

With that simple statement, Dan was promoted
from low man on the list to foreman of the Lazy Q.
Well, Ash had all but given him the title the night
before, he recalled.

"Maybe you can figure out where Keaton's outfit
is taking our cattle," Ash went on.

"I'll keep a lookout," he promised.

"That's all I ask. Meanwhile, if that hombre
you've been watching for comes around, I'll tell him
you're not here and that I ain't seen you. If he wants
to argue about it, I figure that a little buckshot in the
britches ought to persuade him."

Dan chuckled at the mental picture of Ash dis-
patching Draper at the point of a shotgun filled with
buckshot. Then he sobered. He didn't want the
Texas gunfighter hurting innocent people because of
him.

"Draper is supposed to have killed a lot of men,"

he warned. "If he comes around, I hope you'll be careful."

"I intend to do that. With nobody close to enforce the law, a man learns to be careful and to do for himself."

Dan finished eating and strapped on his gun, while Ash gathered the plate, cups, and coffeepot and went back to the house.

At the corral Dan checked on the dun, but before he could get it saddled, a man rode into the clearing. He guessed he must be Aaron Locke. Locke dismounted and gave Dan a puzzled look. He was a gangly fellow, hardly more than a kid. He wore a battered black hat that was a couple of sizes too big. Fortunately, he had an extra large pair of ears that stuck out and kept the hat from sliding down over his face. The effect was comical, and Dan had to suppress a smile.

Ash must have been watching, for he hurried out to greet the newcomer.

"This here is the new foreman, Dan Newland," he announced by way of introduction. "And this is Aaron that I've been tellin' you about."

Aaron's mouth opened into a wide grin, and he stuck out his hand.

"Howdy," he said.

Dan shook his hand.

He noticed that Aaron didn't seem the least bit resentful of his new title and authority. Ash started giving orders, then.

"As soon as Aaron gets some grub under his belt, I want you both to ride back to the others. Be sure and take plenty of ammunition along with you. I wouldn't want you to get caught short.''

The warning wasn't necessary.

Aaron went to the house with his boss to get something to eat, leaving Dan to finish saddling the dun. When he finished, he waited for Aaron to reappear.

''Dan, whenever you're ready, lead the way,'' he said.

When they left, heading north, Ash was watching. Dan was uneasy about leaving the two brothers and Tony alone, but there was nothing else he could do.

All the while, they were gaining in altitude. The evergreens were interspersed with patches of quaking aspens that rattled their leaves in every breeze. Their golden color caught and reflected the light, brightening the whole landscape.

Unlike the Quigley brothers, Aaron wasn't much of a talker. He didn't seem to think it was necessary to fill the void of silence with the sound of his own voice. Since silence had never troubled Dan either, they made a good team, albeit a quiet one. Once when Aaron stopped for a breather, Dan asked him about the other three cowhands that they were on their way to meet.

''There's Kearney, Jacob, and Eloy,'' he said. ''They're all good hands and loyal. After I left, they were going to take a look-around over next to Keaton's range to see if they could find anything suspicious.''

''I take it that's where we're headed now?''

Aaron shoved the oversize hat to the back of his

head, where by some miracle it stayed in place on its own.

"Yeah. I didn't want to say anything to the boss, or to Simon either, and get 'em all stirred up. I figure this is something we can take care of by ourselves."

Dan felt a sense of uneasiness. After the trouble Keaton had with Aaron, he would undoubtedly have his men on alert.

"Ash tells me you had a run-in with some of that outfit awhile back."

"You could call it that," Aaron said. "They caught me looking at one of their brands. It was the Lazy Q burned into that hide, plain as day. When I got back to the ranch, Simon thought it was just the one steer that strayed over where it wasn't supposed to be. But that don't seem too likely to me."

With all the missing cattle to account for, it didn't seem likely to Dan either.

"Anyway," Aaron went on, "I thought they was going to kill me for snooping around, and maybe they would have, but the boys came looking for me. When those hombres found themselves staring down the barrels of three of Mr. Colt's finest products, they lost interest real fast and let me go."

Dan figured it was a good thing that his partners had arrived when they did. Having spent his quota of words, Aaron lapsed into silence once more.

A mountain jay flew across the path of the dun, startling it. While Dan calmed the horse, the bird found a spruce branch to light on. Blue feathers on blue-green made a pretty picture, and he envied the artists who could capture scenes like that with brush and paints. Aaron had stopped up ahead and was waiting for him to catch up.

"It's too bad you didn't get a look at the brands on the rest of that herd," Dan said as if there had never been a pause in the conversation.

"Couldn't. There was so many of Keaton's men that the four of us were satisfied to get out of there without a gunfight."

Dan had to agree with their wisdom. The owner of the Circle K seemed to have everything going his own way—at least for the time being.

"We're not far from last night's camp," Aaron said. "We can track 'em from there."

Sure enough, within the next few minutes they came upon the remains of a campfire. Tracks were all around the place, and the tracks of three horses headed west. They were easy to follow. They led straight toward Keaton's range.

"I hope your friends didn't run into any trouble. We'd better see if we can find them pronto."

He could tell that Aaron was worried too.

"I don't like this, either. They were only going to snoop around a little. They should have been back by now."

Half an hour brought them near to an overlook that would give them a sweeping view of the valley where Aaron had been caught inspecting the steer. They left the horses and made their way to the edge, keeping low so as not to be seen from below should any of Keaton's men still be stationed there. Their caution was justified. Three men were lying on the ground, bound hand and foot, while two guards lounged nearby, smoking and looking bored. There wasn't a cow in sight. The herd had been moved out.

"Looks like the fellows are a little tied up," Aaron whispered.

"The problem is, what do we do about it?"

They backed away quietly to where the horses were waiting. It was obvious they couldn't attack down that steep, barren slope. They'd be shot as easily as geese in a washtub.

"You look like you've got something in mind," Aaron said.

"Maybe. Let's just hope it works."

They stayed among the trees and backtracked to the south where a gentler slope eased down from the ridge some distance away from where the prisoners were being held. There was more cover here, as well. In single file, they made their way to the valley floor. Dan released the thong on his holster and kept his hand close to the gun inside. Because of the formation of the land that formed the ridge, they managed to reach the bottom without being seen. But as they turned back north, one of the guards looked up and spotted them. He dropped his cigarette and yelled a warning.

Once the advantage of surprise was gone, Dan dug his heels into the sides of the dun, causing the great horse to lunge forward. The Colt was now in his hand, ready for use. He could hear Aaron's piebald galloping beside him. A bullet disturbed the air near his ear as it went by. He instinctively threw himself from the saddle, rolling into some clumps of sage for their meager cover. He looked up to see that the piebald was riderless. Then he spotted Aaron on the ground not more than a dozen yards away.

The outlaws had no cover either. Dan leveled the Colt at the one in the red shirt who'd almost severed his ear, and fired. Red Shirt yelped in pain. His partner grabbed the reins of a horse, but it was skittish from the noise of gunfire. The outlaw hopped around on one foot, trying desperately to get the other foot into the stirrup.

Dan and Aaron advanced unchallenged.

"Drop your guns," Dan ordered.

Red Shirt dropped his weapon and raised his hands.

"Don't shoot," he said. "I ain't getting paid enough to die of lead poisoning for anybody."

His partner hesitated, but only for an instant. Then he too surrendered, dropping the reins of the nervous horse.

Dan kept the two covered while Aaron cut the prisoners loose.

"I can't tell you how happy I am that you dropped by," said the big man who sported a dark red beard and a trace of an Irish brogue. "But I'd be happier if you'd done it sooner."

"Keep your britches on, Kearney," Aaron said. "We got here as soon as we could. Besides, you three didn't have to get yourselves into trouble the first minute my back was turned."

Kearney laughed.

"Seems to me that it wasn't all that long ago that we saved your careless, misbegotten hide," he said.

Aaron grinned sheepishly.

"Guess you've got a point."

He turned to Dan.

"I'd better introduce you to the outfit you'll be working with," he said. "This mouthy, ungrateful fellow is Kearney O'Malley. Over there is Jacob Smith, and the quiet one is Eloy Chavez."

Dan nodded to each in turn.

"Boys, meet the new foreman of the Lazy Q. His name is Dan Newland, fresh from Texas."

"Welcome," Kearney said, "it's about time we got a new foreman. I expect my friends, here, agree."

Although neither of them said much, Dan got the impression they felt the same way as the Irishman. He noticed that Keaton's hirelings were watching and listening to everything that was being said.

"Get up," Dan ordered the prisoners.

"What are you going to do?" Red Shirt asked.

Without answering, he tied Red Shirt's hands and told him to get on his horse. When the outlaw was mounted, he fastened his hands to the saddle horn. Next, he did the same to his partner, while the men from the Lazy Q watched approvingly. Red Shirt's wound was superficial but it was obviously causing him some discomfort.

"The boss is going to make you sorry about this," he threatened.

"I expect he'll try," Dan said. "But as far as you two coyotes are concerned, I want you to ride back and tell him that I'm the new foreman who's working for Ash Quigley. Tell him that I won't tolerate him or anybody else laying a hand on any of my men from now on. Tell him that if it ever happens again, I'm going to pay him a visit and put the Lazy

Q brand on his own hide. I'll wager he's familiar with it by now.''

''Then I hope you've got your coffin ready,'' said Red Shirt's partner, ''for the boss is sure going to give you need of it.''

''Let him try. He knows where to find me.''

With that, Dan slapped the horses' rumps and sent them running.

''I believe that's as fine a rescue job as I've ever seen,'' said Kearney, who was busy rubbing the circulation back into his wrists.

''I have to agree,'' Jacob said. ''But if Keaton's foreman, Collins, hadn't insisted on riding back and getting the go-ahead from his boss before killing us, there wouldn't be anything left of us to rescue.''

''And it's too late to retrieve the cattle,'' Eloy said. ''As soon as they caught us, all but the guards and the foreman began moving them out to another place.''

''Looks like we're in the middle of a no-holds-barred war,'' Kearney said, ''and you got here in time to keep us from getting shot with our hands tied behind our backs.''

So Dan had gotten himself into another war. All of a sudden, Draper seemed a lot less important. He marveled at how, in all of the vast Arizona Territory, he'd managed to run across one small buckboard whose occupants would change his life. Maybe this was what his father had called ''fate.''

Jacob and Eloy got the feeling back in their limbs and set about rounding up their mounts, along with Kearney's. Soon the five of them were leaving the valley behind.

When they were back on top of the ridge, Dan asked Jacob to estimate the size of the herd that the outlaws had accumulated.

"About sixty of 'em, I reckon. Maybe more. We had a chance to look at quite a few before they caught us."

"What brands did they wear?"

"A lot of 'em was ours. But some of 'em belonged to Ames Barton. I expected to find some of Captain Timberlake's cattle mixed in too, but didn't see any. Maybe they're afraid of the captain."

"Or maybe they've got his stashed elsewhere," said Kearney, who'd been listening.

Dan figured he might be right.

"I guess it was Aaron's run-in the other day that made you suspicious," he said.

"Well, that," Kearney said, "and the fact that when I was up on the ridge looking the herd over, it occurred to me that I'd seen that ornery, crooked-horn steer down there before. He looked just like the critter that had been such a nuisance among our own. It turned out that I was right. But while we were busy inspecting those brands, Keaton's men swooped down on us, just like they'd been hidden up here all the time, laying for us. I'm ashamed to say that we didn't have a chance to get a single shot fired."

"They hid up on the ridge, among the trees," Jacob said, "and watched until we went into the valley. They weren't on any land that Keaton claims at all. When they attacked, we didn't have the chance of an apple pie at a church picnic."

"We'd better get back to the ranch and let the

Quigleys know what's going on," Dan said. "Simon is going to have to give up his theory of a few solitary steers getting wanderlust."

Kearney chuckled.

"Simon takes a lot of convincing, but I think we can do it."

It was almost dark by the time they got back. Someone had lighted a coal oil lamp and placed it in front of the only window with a glass pane. When they rode up, Ash appeared in the doorway of the stable.

"You're a welcome sight," he said. "But you all look like you've had better days. Did you find any stray cows?"

"Your boys found 'em," Dan said. "Your friend, Keaton, is boarding a whole herd of 'em over at his place."

Ash slapped his thigh.

"Well now, ain't that right neighborly of him. I'd have bet the last dollar I own that Keaton and his no-account outfit were the ones who've been robbing us. I was almost sure of it after the way they done Aaron."

"Sorry that we couldn't bring them home," Keaton said. "But those scoundrels got the drop on us. We were hog-tied, and they'd have shot us just as soon as the foreman got the orders from Keaton, himself. It's a good thing Aaron and Dan came along when they did."

Ash pulled out a bandanna from his back pocket and wiped the sweat from his face, even though there was an evening chill in the air. Tony and

Simon had quietly joined the group in time to hear Kearney's account.

Though it was twilight, Dan noticed that Tony's hands were clenched so tightly that her knuckles were white.

"He's gone too far this time," Ash said. "Cattle rustling is bad enough, but cold-blooded murder is worse."

Dan agreed with him, but the fact was they were on their own, and the odds were against them. As he saw it, they were going to have to put the enemy on the defensive and keep him there. Like a hive of bees, they were going to have to keep stinging and flying away, and then coming back to sting again. Idly he wondered what kind of bees Ames Barton and Captain Timberlake would make.

"Dan, what are we going to do?" Simon asked.

Dan was anxious to get his horse fed and put away for the night. He'd hoped to postpone this talk until daylight, but it wasn't to be.

"I've been studying on the matter," he confessed.

Suddenly all eyes were focused on him, and he felt as uncomfortable as if he were wearing long johns in July.

"I have an idea. Maybe you could call it a plan, or almost a plan. But I need to do some more thinking before we start anything."

"We'll be waitin' to hear then," Ash said.

Tony Quigley's icy stare made Dan feel even more uncomfortable than he already did. He knew as well as anybody that ideas didn't always work the way they were supposed to. A whole lot could go wrong. But he had to do something, or else the Quigleys were going to lose everything they'd worked for.

"Do you really think we've got a chance?" asked Simon, who'd become the worrier.

"It all depends," Dan said. He didn't say on what.

Tony was standing with the last of the light behind her, and she was looking at him like he was the biggest liar in the whole Territory. Well, he admitted to himself, she just might be right about that.

Chapter Three

Noah Keaton paced impatiently in front of the corral while his men saddled fresh horses.

"Don't keep me standing here all day," he shouted.

This was all Collins's fault, he fumed. He'd come slinking in to ask permission to carry out the job he'd been hired to do. The man had no guts or initiative, and not much brains. Now, with almost half the day gone, he was going to have to ride out and see that the job was done right.

He stopped abruptly and leaned against a corral pole, taking some of the weight off his tired feet. A long time ago, he'd realized that he was smarter than most men, and that he had the ability to get things done. But then, you didn't survive on the backstreets of New York if you weren't smart, able, and alert. He was strong too. It wasn't just a muscular strength, either, for his body housed a strong will. It felt good to remind himself of this from time to time.

He was aware that nobody with reasonably good vision would ever call him handsome. His eyes were too small for his face, his hair was thinning rapidly, and his stomach muscles had given way due to Emma's cooking. In fact he'd developed a sizable paunch. Then, too, there was the old knife scar that angled from his chin to his ear, a souvenir of a long-ago knife fight in the Bowery. The enemy who'd drawn his blood had died that day. Unfortunately, Noah still carried the highly visible reminder.

Women preferred good-looking men, he knew that. Certainly all of the beautiful ones did. They paid attention to tall men who had lots of hair and a taut belly. But he'd noticed that most women also liked wealth and power. He intended to have enough of both to offset his liabilities.

There had been gossip around the ranch about how he might soon be marrying Emma, his widowed housekeeper. But that was nonsense. Although she could cook a decent meal, Emma annoyed him. She was totally unsuitable, as well. Instead, he planned to take a bride who was beautiful and cultured—one who'd make other men envious whenever he appeared with her beside him. He smiled at the thought, for one of his greatest desires was to be envied.

He straightened to his full height when he saw Collins approach, leading the powerful California sorrel that had cost him a fortune in Fort Yuma. The stallion's red-gold hide gleamed in the sunlight as it stepped behind the foreman like the true aristocrat that it was.

"He's ready to ride, boss," said Collins, handing over the reins.

Noah took them with a firm grip and hoisted himself into the saddle. The leather squeaked under his weight, and the big horse sidestepped. But once Noah was settled on the sorrel's back, he felt as if he'd grown at least a foot taller and ten years younger. He could imagine that he already had all the things he yearned for—good looks, wealth, power, and breeding. There was no doubt in his mind that the stallion was worthy of every gold piece that he'd paid for it.

"Tell the others that I'm ready to ride," he ordered. "And while you're at it, keep an eye on that new man, Draper. I don't trust him."

"Yes, sir," Collins said. "I was keepin' an eye on him, 'cause I ain't sure but what the Quigleys sent him over here to spy on us."

It irritated him that Collins was pretending to have some initiative. Without another word, he wheeled his mount and rode through the gate, leaving the others to catch up as best they could.

Before he'd gone more than a few hundred yards, he caught sight of two riders coming toward him at full gallop.

"Hey, it's Stipp and Krupski!" someone behind him shouted. "Something's wrong."

Noah and his men rode to meet them. When he got close, he could see that their hands were tied.

"Cut us loose," yelled Krupski, who appeared to be wounded.

His expression was one of fury mixed with pain and embarrassment.

They reined up, and the new man, Draper, threw back his head and roared with laughter.

"This is one for the books," he said as tears rolled down his face.

The others joined in, and Noah could appreciate the humor even though he was disgusted with the two who'd failed him.

Humiliated, Krupski began to swear, using an extensive store of expletives. Stipp satisfied himself with glaring at his tormentors.

"Why are you trussed up like that?" Noah demanded. "And what happened to those nosy cowhands you were supposed to be guarding?"

"None of it was our fault," Stipp whined. "They sneaked up on us and attacked before we could do a thing."

"Who sneaked up on you? I thought you'd captured the whole outfit except for that Locke kid and the Quigleys themselves."

"Locke was one of 'em," Krupski said. "But he had a stranger with him. I ain't never seen him before. He was plenty tough, and he could handle a gun with the best of 'em."

The news troubled Noah.

"I heard that Ash Quigley went to Fort Yuma. Did he go there to hire himself a gunfighter?"

To his surprise, Draper was the one who provided the answer.

"I believe I know the man that he's talking about. He's an old acquaintance of mine from Texas, by the name of Dan Newland. In fact, I've been on his trail for quite a spell, and I was sure that he was holed up around here someplace."

"Never heard of him," Noah said. "Is this Newland fellow as good with a gun as they claim he is?"

Draper snorted in contempt.

"I'll wager that those two never got the chance to find out. My brother did, though. Him and Newland shot it out, and Newland killed him."

Noah stared at him.

"Do you mean to tell me that you don't hold a grudge against the man who shot down your own brother?"

The question made Draper laugh, but it was a mean one that sent chills down Noah's spine.

"I'm not telling you anything of the kind," he replied. "Do you think I came all this way to sip tea with Newland? I intend to fill him full of regrets that he ever heard the name Draper."

Now this was an attitude that Noah could understand. He knew all about vengeance, the settling of scores. This was the true test of a real man, and he was pleased that Draper felt the way he did. Still, the Texan was a stranger who'd wandered in and asked for a job. Noah didn't trust him. For that matter, he didn't trust anyone. But maybe he'd be able to use Draper.

"If you're right about this Newland fellow," he said, "and he's working for the Quigleys, now, it might be that you can have your revenge and get paid for it too."

Draper looked interested, but said nothing. The others watched.

"We'll talk later in private," Noah said.

One of the men reached over and cut the humiliated cowhands loose from their saddle horns.

"Go on to the ranch and wait for me, both of

you,'' Noah ordered. ''I'll have a few things to say to you when I get back.''

Noah wanted to ride, and any excuse would do. Even though the cattle had been moved out, and the prisoners were long gone, he decided to continue on and look over the place where the rescue had been launched. His men followed.

Riding always cleared his head and calmed his nerves. But he soon discovered that today it wasn't working. Pleasure in his magnificent horse had failed him, and somebody was going to pay for that.

At the place near the edge of his land, beneath a high ridge, they stopped. Noah could read from the tracks much of what had happened, even though he was far from an expert. The end of the story was told by the tracks of five riders heading for the top of the ridge. At least they hadn't gone looking for their cattle. Good. There would be time to finish altering the brands, giving them a chance to heal. Then they could be herded off his range entirely, and sold.

Unfortunately, the Quigleys knew for certain what was going on. Even if they couldn't prove what they knew, the other ranchers respected old Ash. They'd believe anything he said. With everyone on their guard, cattle rustling was going to turn into a difficult, risky business—even more so than usual.

Noah reached for his canteen and took a long drink. In this country of low humidity, the dry air sucked the water right out of a man's body. Ever since coming here, Noah was always thirsty.

He glanced over at Collins who wore his usual hangdog look. If the foreman had simply done his job right in the first place, Locke and that Texan would have got here too late, and they wouldn't have found a thing. When the time came, it would give him considerable pleasure to get rid of the bungler.

"You want us to go after 'em?" Collins asked as if sensing that he was in Noah's thoughts.

"Too late for that," he said and growled. "You should have shot 'em when you had the chance."

Noah had the satisfaction of watching Collins turn a shade paler. The others had backed away from him. Knowing that he was in trouble, they wanted no part of it by association. Noah decided to let him stew for a while.

"Let's go back before it gets dark," he said. "There's nothing we can do here."

On the return ride to the ranch, he mulled the situation over. Things had been going well until now, and his current trouble originated from two old men and a scrawny girl. It was ironic that of all the ranchers in the area, he'd considered them the easiest target. A lesson he'd learned on the waterfront, and in the Bowery, was that you started with the most vulnerable, and then you worked your way up from there.

He recalled those days in the city, where he'd started as a youthful pickpocket. From that lowly position, he'd worked his way up to become one of Boss Bentley's lieutenants. He should have been satisfied with his success, but he'd seen the opportunity to do a little skimming. He'd been careful, and the discrepancy was almost impossible to detect. However, he hadn't reckoned with Boss Bentley's eagle eye and suspicious nature. In the end, Noah narrowly escaped New York with his life.

Quite by accident, he'd glanced out the window and spotted two of Boss's enforcers coming for him. He left everything behind and fled. By clinging to the bottom of a trash wagon, he'd made his way to the tracks. A freight car had carried him to safety.

Once he'd started on his journey westward, Noah kept going until he was far beyond Boss's sphere of influence. Distance and time caused changes in him. He felt himself becoming more self-confident, more in control of his life. He no longer had to answer to anyone, and he liked that very much.

During the first year of his travels, he discovered that there was plenty of opportunity for making quick, easy money. It seemed that people were people no matter where they lived, and many of them were easy prey.

Over the years, his scams financed a comfortable life and his ever-westward journey. Finally, his wandering brought him to the Arizona Territory. Always, before, he'd wanted to be on the move. He'd felt safer without roots or ties. But maybe because he was older, he'd grown tired of that kind of life. It was time now for staying put and creating his own domain here in the high country.

On impulse, he nudged the sides of the sorrel and enjoyed the surge of power. The stallion left the others far behind.

The wind whipped his face and shoulders, and he could taste the tiny grains of dirt in his mouth. The strong, smooth-flowing muscles of the horse beneath him gave him a welcome sense of invulnerability. In a mystical way, he felt as one with the creature as it gobbled the land with its strides. Nothing could hold him back. Not Ash Quigley. Not Newland. And not the dunderheads in his employ. He had a renewed vision of his destiny, and he rode confidently toward it.

By the time he arrived at the gate, he was feeling his old self again. He waited for the others and left the horse in their care. As Draper walked past, he stopped him.

"When you hired on, you told me that you were pretty good with a gun," he said. "Is that just a lot of hot air?"

"You want an exhibition?"

Noah decided that, if he was bluffing, it was a good bluff.

"Not now, but when you get through here, I want you to come up to the house. We got some business to discuss."

Draper looked like he was sizing him up, then he nodded.

"I'll be along as soon as I get something to eat."

"Good enough."

Noah was hungry himself, and Emma would be waiting for him. He walked the short distance to the house, pushed open the door, and went inside. The aroma of freshly baked bread greeted him. It filled the whole room.

Emma was busy at the fireplace, where she was stirring something in an iron pot. When she heard his step, she looked up.

"Well, you're back at last, Noah. Your supper's ready. I've been keeping it warm for you."

As usual, she wore a faded calico dress that, at one time, had been bright blue. Wisps of dull brown hair had escaped her bun to fall around her face, creating a frumpy look. In the firelight, he noticed that lines had already formed around her eyes and mouth. Emma's youth was a thing of the past.

Whatever she was cooking smelled good, though, and he was hungry. He pulled out the wooden bench in front of the table and sat down. No sooner had he done so than Emma was at his side with a bowl of venison stew. To that she added a slab of light bread.

"I'll wait around until after you've finished," she said. "Then I'll clean up the dishes."

She reminded him of a feathered, clucking hen. He wasn't pleased. She was always finding reasons to stay close by. But he conceded that she did need to clean up after the meal.

"That's a fine horse you bought yourself down in Yuma," she went on. "Yes sir, a real fine horse, if I do say so myself."

Her attempt to draw him into petty conversation was transparent. Maybe if she was a few years younger, and a whole lot prettier, he'd feel differently about her. But there was no two ways about it, Emma wasn't young and she wasn't pretty.

"Yeah," he replied to her statement about the horse. All the while, he kept his attention focused on his food, for he'd learned that one-word answers eventually discouraged her. Hopefully she'd give up soon and shut up.

His strategy worked, for Emma grew quiet until he finished his stew. But as soon as he put the last spoonful into his mouth, he heard the swishing of her long skirt as she moved across the rough board floor to refill his bowl.

"Heard you was havin' some more trouble with the Lazy Q outfit."

"Umm," he mumbled, for his mouth was still full.

"My Lester knew Asher Quigley real well. He's a canny one. His brother, now, he's soft. There's no starch in him at all. But Asher is a man to look out for."

She was hovering at his elbow as she filled his cup. She smelled like lye soap and sweat all mixed together. The overpowering combination insulted his nose. The woman was vexing him beyond endurance, and without warning, he grabbed her sleeve near where it was attached to the shoulder. It took very little of his strength to pull her down close to his face, but the material of her dress was worn and weak. It ripped at the seam.

"Don't you go poking your nose in where it don't belong," he threatened, "and don't go gossiping all over the place about my business. If I ever find out that you have, I'm going to make you sorry that you was ever born."

She struggled to keep her balance and prevent the hot coffee from spilling. She almost succeeded. Luckily, it splashed onto the table. Had it scalded his hand, he'd have knocked her across the room. He was satisfied with the look of terror in her eyes. It told him that he'd finally gotten through to her.

"I wouldn't think of gossipin'," she protested. "I don't tell nobody nothin' that goes on around here."

He held her for another instant before letting her go.

"Just see that you don't," he warned.

She scurried back to the fireplace and busied herself with the pots and dishes. The torn portion of her sleeve dropped, revealing the pale flesh of her upper arm. With his anger released, Noah was able to finish the rest of his meal in as near a condition of contentment as he was able to feel.

He wished there wasn't such a scarcity of women in the West. Men had to be less choosy. That is, if they could be choosy at all. After Emma's husband, Lester Huffman, had been trampled in a stampede, she'd asked for a job keeping house for him, and he'd obliged. That she was interested in more than just a job soon became apparent. He liked her cooking well enough, but she wasn't the woman for him. Her waist had thickened, her features were coarse, and she slumped and shuffled. She was past thirty and she looked it. He never encouraged her, but that didn't matter to Emma. The woman had no pride.

When she finished with her work, Emma slipped out the door to go to her own little cabin a short walk away. He was relieved to be rid of her.

Noah left the table and dropped his bulk into the big hide-covered chair with a sigh. It had a rich leather smell that he liked. Outside of a saddle, this chair was where he felt the most comfortable He reached over and helped himself to a cigar from a box that sat on a nearby stand. He enjoyed a good smoke as much as anyone, and the cigars were one of his favorite indulgences.

He thought of Draper and wondered what was

keeping him. Surely the man had his belly full of beans by now. As if in response to his thought, there was a knock at the door.

"Come in," he called.

Draper's form filled the doorway.

"I'm here. Speak your piece."

The man was arrogant, and Noah hated arrogance in his hired hands. Later, he was going to have to do something about that.

"Have a seat," he invited, keeping his voice friendly.

Draper sauntered over and perched on the corner of the table that faced the leather chair.

"You got another one of them cigars?" he asked.

Noah took one from the box and tossed it to him. His cigars were expensive and hard to come by, but he'd go along with Draper for a while since the gunman could well be the solution to one of his problems—although, to him, Draper didn't look all that impressive. He wasn't a big man, just average. He looked old enough to have garnered some experience, but he wasn't too old. Noah would never have picked him out on the street as being a fast gun. But one never could tell.

"Are you serious about settling your score with the Newland fellow?" Noah asked. "Or were you just talking?"

"I'm serious, and I'll take care of him in my own time, and in my own way."

Draper cut off the end of his cigar and lit it.

"I've got a proposition for you, then. If you'll hurry up and do the job right, I'll pay you a hundred dollars. You needn't meet him face-to-face, either.

I'm not paying a bonus for giving him an even chance.''

Noah watched as the gunman puffed away. Surrounded by a cloud of smoke, Draper seemed to be considering the offer.

''Make it a hundred and fifty,'' he said at last.

Noah nearly dropped his own cigar into his lap. Draper had plenty of brass. He'd give him that.

He started to protest, but instead, he eased back into his chair. Why quibble with this saddle bum? What was fifty more dollars to him anyway? It was well worth that much to get rid of Newland and the threat he represented.

''It's a deal,'' he said. ''But I don't want any mistakes. I want Newland dead—and soon.''

Draper looked at him through a haze of smoke with squinting eyes.

''I'll take half now, and the other half when the job's done.''

''Fair enough.''

Noah hauled himself up from the chair and walked over to the fireplace. There, he drew out a tin box that had been hidden behind some books on the mantle. He opened the lid and began to count bills.

''Hold it,'' Draper ordered. ''You can put that paper right back where you got it. I want my payment in gold.''

Noah stared at him.

''What makes you think that I got any?''

Draper laughed.

''What do you take me for? A man like you has always got gold stashed away.''

Noah was alarmed. The fact that a loaded derringer lay on the mantle just inches away from his hand didn't help a bit. To touch that gun would mean his death. He'd grown accustomed to dealing with dullards like Collins, but Draper was of a different breed. Draper was dangerous.

"I'm not about to show you where I keep my gold."

Draper stood up and backed toward the door.

"That's okay with me. Just bring the agreed-on amount to me right before sunup. I'll be waiting for you on this side of the bunkhouse."

He left then, walking out into the evening, still surrounded by the smoke of Noah's expensive, imported cigar.

Noah shoved the box back into its hiding place. He felt like he'd lost control, and he didn't like the feeling. It irked him to have to use part of his gold cache for payment. Most of all he didn't like Draper. Maybe he'd find a way to get rid of Draper too, when his usefulness was over. After all, it would only take one accurately placed bullet.

It was just before dawn when Noah made his way across the open space that separated his dwelling from the bunkhouse. He carried the bag of gold pieces under one arm. The whole landscape was draped in gray, broken by dark shadows. Involuntarily he shivered. There was no sign of Draper anywhere. He called out his name softly, and was startled when the gunman came up behind him as silently as a cat.

"Have you got it?" he asked Noah.

Without a word, Noah handed over the gold.

Draper made a big show of hefting the bag.

"It's got a nice feel to it. Real nice. It's about the right weight too."

"Half now, half later," said Noah, trying to recover his poise after letting the gunman sneak up on him. "Just make sure that you earn it."

Draper's response was measured and deadly

"Look here, Keaton, nobody questions my ability, and nobody tells me how to do my job. If it turns out that you have any complaints, you can strap on a gun and explain 'em to me later in front of this bunkhouse."

For the first time since his escape from New York, Noah felt real gut-wrenching fear. Draper wasn't a man he could buy. He was a rattlesnake, loyal only to himself, and coiled to strike. Noah realized he'd gone too far. His hands were clammy and a trickle of sweat rolled down the side of his face.

"Look, I didn't mean anything by what I said. I don't want any trouble. Do the job however you see fit, and the rest of the payment will be waiting for you when you're done."

There was an interminable silence before Draper spoke.

"Fine," he said then. "We're in agreement."

Noah backed away, just as he would have backed off from a poisonous snake. In doing so, he felt humiliated. When he took his eyes off the shadowy form of Draper for a second, the gunman disappeared. Noah heaved a sigh of relief, and then he practically sprinted the rest of the distance to the safety of the house. On the way, he passed Emma's darkened cabin, scarcely noticing it.

He didn't know how fast Newland was with a gun, but it really didn't matter anymore. With all the money he was being paid, Draper could put his pride in his pocket and shoot Newland from ambush.

Noah's nerves were quieter by the time he reached the door. He remembered his old rule. When you have a problem you deal with it. He'd learned this early on. And if the solution to the problem becomes a problem, then you deal with that too. Boss Bentley hadn't trained any dumb lieutenants, and Noah Keaton wasn't dumb.

Before he stepped inside, he noticed a blush of pink creeping up from the eastern horizon. It would soon sweep the grayness away. This was going to be a fine day, he decided. He was going to make certain of that.

Chapter Four

The ranch was far behind him now as Dan rode north again. This time he was alone. The others had been left behind to do their work and defend the place if need be. Keaton's dominance had been threatened by the rescue of their men, and Dan doubted if he'd let that threat go unchallenged.

Meanwhile, he'd set out to find the valley where Aaron suspected the stolen cattle were being held. If and when he found it, he'd do whatever he could, depending on the number of outlaws who were with the herd.

The morning was still fresh as the dun made its way through the heavily scented pines as silently as a ghost. Dan didn't want to advertise his whereabouts in case Keaton had some of his men scouting the area.

The air was cool and thin; the filtered sunshine had almost a mystical quality. Nature had been generous to this verdant plateau, so rich in animal and plant life. He rode quietly, enjoying the company of his own thoughts. He wasn't sure just when he began to sense that he wasn't alone. The feeling was subtle at first, growing in intensity. It was much the same as knowing when someone else is present in a dark room. Suddenly, he guided the dun into a thick stand of pines that would hide him from the view of anyone who followed. Here he waited.

He heard a twig snap under the weight of a hoof. His body tensed, ready for action. He drew the .45.

A lone rider came into view. His head was lowered as he looked for signs of Dan's trail. On his head was a familiar weather-beaten hat, and beneath him was the roan that Ash favored. The old man had followed him. Dan was angry. He rode directly into the roan's path.

Ash pulled up, startled by his sudden appearance.

"What do you mean, scaring me half to death like that!" he cried. "And why are you tagging along? I thought we'd agreed that I was to go alone."

Ash shoved his hat to the back of his head and looked Dan square in the eyes.

"I know I made you foreman, and I think it's an even better idea now, than I did when I first got it. But make no mistake. I still own this outfit. There's plenty of men back there to take care of things, and you need to have somebody ride shotgun for you."

Ash was a stubborn old buzzard, Dan would give him that, and there was sense to what he said.

"Okay, you win. But just so you know it, I'm against your coming along."

Ash grinned at the concession.

"Knowed you was smart the first time I met you."

Smart didn't exactly describe the way Dan felt.

58 S. J. Stewart

"Let's get going, then, if you've a mind to."

He took off again for the north, this time with Ash beside him. The old-timer was uncharacteristically quiet. After they'd covered a lot of ground, he spoke up, sounding worried.

"Son, I ain't seen hide nor hair of any of them owlhoots all morning. I figured that Keaton would have his line patrolled from here to the peaks."

The peaks were many miles away, but the exaggeration was apt.

"Could be that we just haven't run into 'em yet, or maybe they're busy somewhere else."

"Then I hope our luck holds out," Ash said.

So did Dan.

He followed the directions Aaron had given him, and they rode the length of a long ridge to its northernmost end. Having gone as far as they could, they turned westward, descending into a narrow valley. Dan marveled at how different this part of the country was from the desert he'd crossed only days before. There was no sign of hostile Indians that he could see, but then they'd been keeping busy far to the south.

They were well into the valley when Ash stopped abruptly. Dan glanced over to see what was wrong. His partner raised his hand and pointed. A short distance away a magnificent bull elk was framed against the trees. The huge creature just stood there as if posed, for he hadn't caught their scent yet. Power and grace were embodied in bone, sinew, and hide. A sudden wind shift betrayed their presence, and with a single leap, the elk disappeared among the trees as if it had been a wraith.

Dan realized that he was holding his breath, and he let it out slowly.

"I think that's got to be just about the purtiest thing the Creator ever made," Ash said.

"I expect it ranks right up there at the top of the list," Dan agreed.

He was thinking of Tony, who was graceful and lovely almost in spite of herself. In a way, there was a wild innocence about her that matched that of the elk.

The moment had passed and they rode on.

They slept under the stars, and it was the afternoon of the following day when they came upon the place they'd been searching for.

It was a fertile range that was large enough to graze many cattle. Dan estimated about sixty were grazing at the moment. Jacob's count was right. He spotted Kearncy's crooked-horn steer that had wandered off to one side. Two of Keaton's men had been assigned to watch the stolen herd.

"I wonder if they've had a chance to change the brands yet," Ash said in a hushed voice.

"Doubt if they've had time since they moved them. But I expect they're planning on it."

"What are we going to do about those two hombres that are nursemaiding 'em?"

Dan shifted his weight in the saddle.

"I reckon we'll have to be neighborly and ride over and say 'howdy.' "

"I guess it wouldn't be polite to keep 'em waiting then."

They drew their sidearms and galloped toward the herd. The rustlers weren't expecting any trouble.

They were smoking and woolgathering instead of watching. It was the sound of hoofbeats that alerted them.

"McLaren!" the nearest one shouted, while with one flowing motion he grabbed his pistol and fired at Ash. In his haste he was careless, and the bullet went wild, but the report roused the herd. As one, they were bawling and stamping their hooves.

The man who'd sounded the alarm was on the outer edge, but McLaren wasn't so lucky. He was in trouble, and he knew it. He had to get himself out of harm's way and leave his partner to fight alone.

Kearney's steer had enough of gunfire. Dan watched as he took out like the devil was after his tail. The others followed his lead.

The outlaw who'd shot at Ash aimed to take another, but Ash was watching McLaren and didn't see the danger. Dan had veered off to the side, and there was no time to shout a warning, even if it could be heard. He raised the Colt and fired. Despite the dust that was being raised, he managed to hit the mark. The man fell from his horse.

McLaren had freed himself from the stampeding animals and had turned back. But it didn't look to Dan like he was going to surrender, probably because the short life of a cattle rustler didn't hold many comforts before the rope. McLaren would figure he had to kill them both. There was a further exchange of gunfire, and Dan felt a jolt, as if someone had punched him in the side. But after the initial impact, there wasn't any pain. Then, as he tried to hold the gun steady, Ash's bullet cut McLaren down.

Dan was starting to think that he'd only imagined

getting hit, when the world around him began to spin. He grabbed hold of the saddle horn and struggled to stay seated, but the dizziness was overwhelming. Through a haze, he saw Ash coming toward him. Then he was falling. The impact sent a shock wave of agony through his body. That first respite of numbness was gone now, and searing pain swept everything else from his consciousness.

He tried to raise himself on one arm, but it collapsed under his weight. Before he could try again, Ash was cradling his head.

"You just lie still, boy. You're goin' to be all right. I'll see to it."

Dan tried to speak, but forming words took too much effort. And besides, he was cold—all except for that spot of fire in his side. Chills wracked his body. One after another, they washed over him in waves. He was convinced that if he didn't die of the bullet wound, he would surely die of the cold.

After an eternity, he felt a blanket being wrapped around him. It helped, but not enough to stop his misery. He could hear Ash building a fire close by. He turned his head to the side and watched the flames leap upward. He was so cold that he wished he could throw his body into the center of that hot light. Maybe in its warmth, the icy waves would stop.

Ash gently lifted his head. In his right hand, he held a cup.

"Dan, swallow as much of this as you can," he urged. "There's nothing better for shock than hot tea. I learned that a long time ago, and I never ride out without some of it in my saddlebags."

Dan tried to drink. At first, the hot liquid merely dribbled down his throat, leaving a trail of blessed warmth. But soon he managed to swallow. When he'd emptied the cup, Ash gently cleaned his wound. Then he packed it to stop the bleeding.

"Well, it looks like you got off lucky this time, son. That bullet passed clean through, so I don't have to be pulling any lead out of you. But just the same, the wound needs to be cauterized."

Dan knew what was coming. The first time he'd seen it done was when his father was caring for a shot-up cowhand. Later, during the war, he'd done it himself. He also knew about the danger of infection if the procedure wasn't followed.

Ash went over to his saddlebags and pulled out a whiskey bottle.

"This ought to help a mite," he said as he held the bottle to Dan's mouth.

Dan took a long swallow. He choked as it stung his throat on the way down. The whiskey was supposed to numb the brain so that a man didn't feel anything. He figured it would take more than what was in that bottle to numb what he was feeling, let alone what he was about to feel.

Again, Ash pulled aside Dan's shirt, and he carefully removed the blood-soaked padding. Dan watched as he took the big hunting knife from his belt and put the broad blade into the fire.

"It's got to be done," the old man said.

Dan steeled himself for the ordeal. Ash leaned over him and pressed the hot blade against the wound. Pain seared through his body, and a groan escaped from clenched teeth. His face was suddenly bathed in sweat, and he was no longer cold. Then there was nothing. . . .

Chapter Five

After a time, Dan broke through the murky silence to regain consciousness. Not all at once, but little by little. When at last he opened his eyes, it was dark. His mouth felt like a pair of old flannel underwear, and there was a pain in his side. Slowly he turned his head and saw that the campfire had burned itself down to remnants. Ash was just beyond it, resting his head against a saddle. His rifle was beside him.

Dan tried to speak, but only managed a croaking sound. He tried again.

"You got any water?" he asked weakly.

Ash was roused from his nap. He came over and looked at Dan.

"Thank the Almighty," he said. "I was worried about you, son. Done all I could, and that was little enough."

"I'm obliged for your help. Guess you were right about me needing somebody to ride shotgun."

He was glad that Ash had been here. The old man

had a lot of common sense whenever he chose to use it, as well as a lot of know-how.

Ash knelt and put a canteen to Dan's lips. The few sips of water helped to dispel the flannel dryness.

"Thought you'd like to know, Dan, that both of them coyotes is dead. They won't be causin' us any more trouble. Now, you just rest and get better."

The two rustlers had been taken care of, but he was aware that there would be plenty more coming to change the brands on the cattle. Ash would know this, as well.

Dan tried to sit up, but he was too weak. His left side throbbed. Gently he explored the area with his fingers and found the bleeding had stopped. A good sign.

Ash stood watching him.

"You lost some blood, but not enough to matter a whole lot. You're young and tough."

That was laughable. Dan felt anything but tough. All he wanted to do was sleep.

When he awoke again, it was fully daylight. He rolled to the left, shifting his weight and putting pressure on the wound. The stab of pain caused him to moan. He lay back and found himself looking into the bright blue eyes of Tony Quigley. He wondered if he was still dreaming.

"Are you real?" he asked, reaching out.

"As real as can be," she said.

"How?"

She reached down and brushed the hair from his forehead with her fingertips.

"I followed Grandpa when he followed you. Two can play at any game, you know, and I'm not his granddaughter for nothing. I had a hunch you'd both get into trouble, and I was right."

"Here," said Ash, who'd come up to his bed and handed him a cup, "try to get some of this down."

Dan propped himself up on his good side and took a taste. Ash had boiled pieces of dried meat, along with wild onions, to make a kind of broth. There were other things in the concoction too, but Dan didn't ask what they were. When he'd drained the cup, he felt a little better. He struggled to get to his feet, and Tony was instantly beside him, steadying him with her arm.

"It's too soon for you to be moving around like this," she warned. "It's only been a couple of days since you got yourself shot."

He wasn't sure that he'd heard her right. Had she said a couple of days? Had he lost a whole day and part of this one?

He noticed that the herd had wandered back, preferring the rich grazing at this end of the valley.

"Have you checked their brands?" he asked Ash.

"Yep. They're divided about even between the Triple B and us. I figure Ames Barton is going to be glad to get his back."

Dan managed a few steps, but he was still weak. He was sure that would pass. At any rate, he'd be able to sit a horse and herd cattle. Leastwise, he was going to give it a try.

"We'd better get these animals out of here before any unfriendly company shows up with six-shooters," he said.

"I don't think you can ride in your condition," said Tony, who'd withdrawn her support, leaving him to stand alone.

"Bet on it," he replied, more to reassure himself than Tony.

"It don't matter cause we ain't leavin' until morning," Ash said. "We've risked staying here this long, we can risk a few more hours."

Tony looked pleased like she'd just won a poker hand.

"Maybe by morning you can actually haul your backside into a saddle," she said.

He conceded that maybe they were right. Another night of rest might make a big difference.

Ash took a look at his wound and put another dressing on it. Afterward, Dan leaned back, exhausted from the effort. Tony came over and sat beside him.

"I really don't know much about you," she said.

He'd noticed that instead of the baggy pants he was accustomed to seeing her wear, she had donned a riding skirt. That, and everything else she had on, fit real well too. Her clothes served to present Tony in a way that nearly took his breath away. And right now, he didn't have any to spare.

"There's not a whole lot to know," he replied to her query. "My mother died when I wasn't much more than an infant, and my father brought me up in Texas."

"Then we have something in common. Only both of my parents died. Grandpa and Uncle Simon filled in for them."

He couldn't help being aware that she smelled like

flowers, and that he liked having her close to him this way.

"They did real well," he observed, glancing at her just long enough to make her blush.

"I guess so. But Grandpa is awfully strict and set in his ways."

He figured that her candor was due to the fact that Ash had ridden off to check the valley, and he couldn't possibly hear what she said.

"He is set in his ways," Dan agreed, "but maybe his strictness builds character."

She laughed.

"Whose? His or mine?"

Dan found himself chuckling.

"Maybe both. My pa was strict too. He believed that whatever we did had consequences that we had to accept. According to him we need to live with that in mind.

"I remember a story he told me about two fellows who were lost. They wandered about in the forest for a long time before they came to a clearing. In the middle of the clearing stood a scaffold that someone had recently constructed. 'Thank goodness,' said one of the fellows. 'We've found our way back to civilization at last.' Pa told me that this was a parable about consequences being taken for granted in a civilized society."

Tony made a face of disgust.

"I hardly think a gallows is a sign of civilization."

"I didn't either, at the time. But Pa explained that the gallows is a statement of respect for life. It says, loud and clear, that the community is going to require the lives of killers, other than in cases of defense of life or property.''

She reached out and touched his hand.

''But you've killed,'' she said.

Somehow he'd known this was coming.

''Yes, I have. At first, it was in the war. Then, whenever I've had to. I accept the consequences.''

''And what have those been?''

He hesitated, wondering if he should tell her, but she was looking at him expectantly with those deep blue eyes.

''I had bad dreams for a long time after the war,'' he said. ''They were so real that I'd wake up sweating in the night. Then after Tate forced me into a shoot-out, I couldn't go back to living the quiet life that I'd made for myself. Sonny Draper came along and wanted to have a go at me because I'd been good enough to kill Tate, but most likely I wasn't fast enough to take him down too. So I had to kill, again. Now Ben Draper is after me for killing Sonny. Who knows how many more are out there who are just like him. This gun dueling thing is a trap, and no matter how hard I try, I can't seem to find a way out of it.''

''I see,'' she said simply, staring at the folded hands in her lap.

''That's why I'm really here,'' he said. ''To get my life back.''

She stayed beside him for a few more minutes without saying another word. Then she got up and walked away. As he watched the gentle sway of her riding skirt, he felt a tiredness sweeping over him that, until now, had simply been lurking. His eyelids grew heavy, and soon he slept.

At morning light he awoke and found that he was feeling a lot stronger. He said as much to Ash.

"That's mighty good news," said the old man, "for we need to round up this herd and get it out of here as fast as we can. We've pressed our luck about as far as anyone ought to. Keaton's crew is apt to be coming up here any time now, to change those brands."

"Here," Tony said, "drink this and you'll feel better."

He took the cup from her hands and drank its contents. It warmed his insides.

"Just let me get my boots on, and I'll be ready to ride," he assured her.

Ash had saddled the dun, and he brought it over. Dan grasped the reins and struggled to mount. His wound gave him pain when he moved too much or too suddenly. Some of the dizziness he'd felt had returned, as well. When he was safely in the saddle, he wondered if he'd be able to stay there. He didn't relish falling on his face in front of an audience, especially Tony Quigley. But after a few deep breaths, his head began to clear.

He noticed that Tony appeared to know what she was doing as she and her grandfather bunched the herd. She was going to be a big help.

Dan rode drag as they drove the small herd eastward. At the same time, he took care to watch for any sign of Keaton's men. When they began their climb out of the valley, Ash dropped back to ride beside him.

"How are you doing?"

"Fine," he assured him. "Eatin' the dust of these cows beats layin' around staring at the sky."

Ash grinned at his answer.

"Glad to see that you're keeping your sense of humor. But it's going to get tougher from now on with the valley behind us. Think you'll be okay?"

Dan nodded. He was aware that he looked bad, but as long as he could stay on the dun, he could work. He'd been through tough times before, and he knew the secret was to keep his mind focused on the job. Once they'd gotten the herd, and themselves, to a safer place he could take it easy for a while and let his wound heal itself. Between now and then, they had a lot of area to cover, and outlaws to watch for.

They'd been traveling for some time before Ash decided to stop. Dan was relieved, for he'd gone about as far as he could without rest. He found himself a place in the shade while Ash built a fire and made coffee. When it was done, Tony brought him a cup, and then she seated herself across from him. She smoothed her skirt and tucked her legs beneath her. Bad as he felt, he was strongly aware of her attractiveness. Idly he wondered what she'd done with those oversize britches she'd worn in the past. In spite of the tension that was so often between them, he found that he liked her a great deal. Maybe, he admitted to himself, what he felt was more than just liking.

"Won't Simon and the others be worried about you?" he asked her.

"No, I left a note on the bunkhouse door telling

them where I was going, which is more than Grandpa did.''

''Then they'll be concerned about him.''

''No they won't, I told them I was following him.''

And that was that as far as she was concerned. The Quigley family was a strange lot. He'd planned to do this on his own and to keep them out of it. But he'd underestimated Ash's bullheadedness, not to mention that of his granddaughter.

When Ash had finished eating, he got to his feet.

''If it's all the same to you, it's time we got started again. The more distance we put between ourselves and that valley, the better I'm going to feel.''

Dan got to his feet with more steadiness than he'd expected. He was moving with greater ease now, and the dizziness was gone. In fact, when he was safely in the saddle, he noted that it felt good to be there.

In the early afternoon, they came to a shallow draw. It was like getting a present. The draw channeled the herd quickly, without obstruction. Once they got them started, Dan rode out to have a look around. The last thing he wanted was to get caught unawares. He saw nothing amiss, however, other than a squirrel scampering along a branch. He was about to rejoin the others when he caught a glimpse of a moving shadow. It was followed by the light skin tone of a human hand. Dan grabbed his rifle and charged.

The rider bolted from cover. He headed in the direction of the Circle K like demons were after his shirttail. For a brief time, Dan followed, but a sharp pain in his side reminded him of his wound. Besides, he couldn't leave Ash and Tony to fend for themselves. He stopped and watched as the outlaw disappeared from sight. When he got back, the others were waiting.

"You did the right thing letting him go," Ash said. "You're not in any shape to be hunting two-legged varmints."

"Especially not since you've got all these ornery four-legged ones that you have to nursemaid," Tony agreed.

He knew she was right, but he wished he could have stopped the man before he got back to his boss. There would be a check, now, on the men Ash had buried in the valley, and they would know the herd had been retrieved. Dan didn't want to think about what Keaton would do in the light of that news.

"Let's get movin' toward home," he said, aware of the beauty of that word he rarely used anymore.

The draw was like a well-surfaced road, and they made good time. Before it ended, it had taken them a long way. By then, it was almost dark.

"You look all tuckered out, son," Ash said as he rode back to see how Dan was holding up. "It's time we made camp."

Dan was glad to oblige. He felt like he'd been riding for a week instead of just a day. His strength was a little slow making a comeback.

Again, they settled for jerky and coffee. That was okay with Dan. He was too tired to eat anyway. Ash must have noticed.

"I'll take the first watch while you get some rest, son," he offered.

Dan didn't argue. He spread out his bedroll in the

darkness, well away from the light of the fire. He crawled into it, thankful for the chance to rest all the parts of his tired, aching body for at least part of the night. When he was drifting off to sleep, someone called, "Hello the camp!"

His hand slid toward the pistol at his side.

"Come on in, boys," Ash said.

Aaron and Kearney walked their horses into the circle of firelight.

"Thought it was about time for us to come lookin' for you," Aaron said. "We expected you back sooner, and thought you might be needin' some help."

"Got slowed down a little," Ash said. "But we're doin' fine, now."

"It appears to me that you are," Kearney said. "You've picked up a whole blooming herd somewhere."

"The nice thing about it," Tony said from the rim of darkness, "is that most of it is ours."

Aaron gave a low whistle.

"Good work," he said. "But what about Dan? He doesn't look too spry."

Dan was still under the covers, quietly listening.

"Afraid he had a run-in with a couple of no-accounts who work for the Circle K. They didn't like us dropping in on 'em, and they got plumb nasty."

"What Grandpa means," Tony said, "is that Dan got shot. He's got a hole in his side, and he lost some blood."

"I'm fine," he said. "I tried to duck, but I just wasn't fast enough."

Kearney laughed at his attempt at humor.

"A man's got to learn. I expect you'll know to be faster next time."

"Maybe you could use a couple of extra hands moving these animals," Aaron said. "It'd be a shame to miss out since we're already at the party."

"We can use all the help you can give us," Ash said.

He threw some pieces of wood on the fire and watched it flame up. Then he put some coffee on to boil.

"Take a load off your feet," he said to the newcomers. "Tomorrow is going to be a workday."

Dan was listening with his eyes closed, and that was the last thing he remembered. That and the smell of coffee.

No one shook him awake to ask him to stand watch, and when he opened his eyes it was almost daylight. Thankfully, the pain in his side had diminished to nothing more than a dull throb. He remembered that Keaton would know, by now, about the raid on the valley. The question was, what would the outlaw do about it? Would he come after the herd, believing it to be poorly defended? Would he send someone to check on the men he'd left guarding the cattle? Would he bide his time before he attacked the Lazy Q?

Aaron was standing watch, and Dan went over to him.

"Is anyone at the ranch with Simon?"

"Yes. Jacob is with him. He's a good man, and can make the decisions that Simon can't. Eloy is guarding what's left of the herd. We're holding it on rangeland northeast of the ranch."

Their manpower was spread too thin, and Dan didn't like it. While they were breaking camp, Dan told them about his concerns.

"How would you play this hand?" Ash asked.

"I'd have you, Tony, and Kearney go back to the ranch. That will leave Aaron and me to take the shortcut with the herd. We'll leave them with Eloy and head for the ranch ourselves."

"You're worried about our house," Tony said. "Do you really think that sidewinder would attack?"

Dan turned to her.

"Do you think for one minute that he wouldn't?"

She dropped her gaze, and he had his answer.

After the ones who were going to the ranch took their leave, he and Aaron started the herd to moving. Just in case Keaton had decided to follow, he wanted to put as much distance between himself and the enemy as possible.

When they stopped for a breather, Aaron rode back to him.

"Just wanted to tell you, Dan, that I think you've got things going in the right direction. It was bothersome to have to watch Ash and Simon being stolen blind, and not be able to do anything about it."

Dan tipped back his hat and wiped the sweat from his forehead. Was it such a short time ago that he'd been freezing?

"I'm not sure exactly what it is that I've started," he said. "But I know that Keaton is the kind who won't quit until he has everything he can lay his hands on. At some point, somebody is going to have to stand up to him. It might as well be us, and it might as well be now.''

Aaron climbed down from the piebald and sat with his back against a tree.

''That's the way I've been thinking for quite a spell, but Simon is gun-shy. Then there was Ash with that bee in his bonnet to get Tony out of here and back east. None of us wanted him to go, and Tony sure as blazes didn't. But he risked their lives so that Tony could stay with the wife of a lieutenant and go to Pennsylvania with her when the husband got the transfer he was expecting. The woman is some kind of shirttail relative is how Ash knew about her.''

This was answering some of the questions that Dan had about their reckless journey.

''What went wrong?'' he asked, for something obviously had.

''Fate, I guess. Ash got there a few days late. The orders had come early, and the lieutenant and his wife had to leave. That old man was sure disappointed, but Tony wasn't. She claimed she didn't care anything about dressing up in crinolines and sipping tea from china cups in somebody's drawing room. Ash almost had to hog-tie her to get her to go to Yuma in the first place.''

Dan tried to imagine Tony all gussied up, making polite murmurs at an Eastern tea party. The image failed. Instead, he saw her in a riding skirt, her hair falling loose around her shoulders. Instead of polite conversation, she'd be giving orders to everyone within earshot. This was the Tony he knew and cared about. Then he thought of Keaton.

"Maybe it would have been better for her if Ash's plan had worked out."

"Maybe. But I don't think Tony would have missed this show for anything. I think she's real glad to be back home."

As soon as the horses were rested, they started on. They pushed hard, for Dan wanted to deliver the herd and get back to the ranch house with the others. He hated to leave Eloy alone, but there was no sign that they were being followed. His gut instinct told him that it was the ranch that Keaton would target.

There was no two ways about it, they needed more men, and getting them was his responsibility. He was going to have to work on that.

When they approached, Eloy heard them coming.

"*Madre de Dios*," he exclaimed. "Are those ours? Where did you find them?"

"About half of 'em belong to us," Dan said. "The rest have the Barton brand. We found 'em stashed in that valley where Aaron thought they'd likely be."

"Are none of *Señor* Timberlake's cattle among them?"

"I'd have bet on it," Aaron said, "but maybe Keaton's not so eager to rile the captain."

"He might be holding off the Timberlake place for a while."

If so, Dan doubted that he'd hold off forever. Greed was a strong goad, and from what he'd heard, the TL brand offered an opportunity that was too good to pass up.

"We're leaving these with you. Since we weren't followed, I expect there's going to be trouble back at the ranch. As soon as we can, we'll let Barton know what's going on, and he can send someone to take his share.''

Eloy nodded.

"I'll take care of them."

They left him with his work and headed for the house. It was almost dark when they caught sight of it. He was relieved to see that nothing had happened in his absence.

"You made good time," said Ash, who proceeded to usher them to the table as soon as they got there.

Ash cooked the latecomers two large venison steaks and put the plates before them. For the first time since he'd been wounded, Dan had an appetite. He noticed that Ash was watching as he made the steak disappear.

"Son, I know for a fact that you're on the mend if you can eat like that."

Dan managed a grin. He had to agree, for the pain was almost gone, and the wound was beginning to itch, which he'd heard was a good sign.

"What do we do now?" Tony asked as she leaned over to fill Aaron's coffee cup. "Do we just sit here like nice little mice waiting for the big tomcat Keaton to pounce on us? Or maybe we should declaw him."

It seemed to Dan that Tony sounded downright aggressive. He could understand her frustration; waiting around for Keaton to pounce wasn't his idea of fun either. A long time ago his father had told him that sometimes the best defense is an attack. As he saw it, they'd made a beginning at an offensive by taking back what was theirs. Now he intended to stay on the offensive. It was going to be hard, though, with so few men. He needed to recruit allies, and the first thing he planned to do was talk to Barton. After that, he'd ride over and see if he could persuade Captain Timberlake that he too had a stake in this war against the rustlers. With those two for allies, they just might have a fighting chance,

In any event, he needed to let Ames Barton know that some of his cattle had been recovered, for no rancher could afford to lose that many.

"My dear, I want you to quit worrying yourself about this Keaton business," said Simon, who'd come in shortly after the steaks were done. "It just won't do you any good, and it'll put wrinkles in your face."

When her uncle turned then to fill his cup, Tony made a face at him that would have been a tragedy if it had frozen in place. But when he turned back, her countenance was angelic once more.

"A stranger might get the impression that I didn't have a share in this ranch, Uncle Simon," she complained, casting a glance at Dan, whom she must have regarded as the "stranger."

"Just hold on now, Missy," Ash said. "Nobody here said you don't have your part in this place. Of course you do, and you do your share of work too."

Ash's conciliatory words seemed to have little effect on his granddaughter. While they watched, she did an about-face and marched over to the sleeping area at the other end of the house. With a flick of the wrist, she disappeared behind the curtains.

Dan figured that Tony's sleeping quarters was likely as good a place as any for her to cool off her temper. Besides, he sympathized with her feelings. She did more work and had more spunk than her uncle had.

He finished the last few bites of venison and drained the cup of its contents. Then he got up from the table.

"I know we're expecting trouble, but it's important that I ride out in the morning and talk to a couple of your neighbors. Barton needs to be told about his cattle, and I'm going to ask him and Timberlake to join with us against Keaton. As sure as sin, he's their enemy too."

Ash leaned back as if he was studying on something.

"It occurred to me a little while ago," he said, "that you might have it in your mind to go calling on Barton and the captain for just such a reason. Now, Ames Barton is a good man. Nobody's going to dispute that. But you'd better know that the captain is a strange one. He keeps to himself, and it ain't likely that he'll be wanting to join up with us. I spoke to him once about a matter that should have been of mutual interest. He acted arrogant as blazes and said that he'd take care of his own business and I could jolly well take care of mine."

Dan didn't like the sound of it. Maybe Ash was right. Maybe riding all the way to talk to Timberlake would be a waste of time. But they were in a war, and the outcome was crucial to all the ranchers in this part of the Territory. Maybe the captain could be persuaded to step off his pedestal and take part in the real world. At any rate, Barton sounded like a reasonable man, one who'd join with his neighbors and put up a good fight for his property.

"You know me by now," he told Ash. "I'm one of the hardheaded Newlands, so I guess I'll have to find out for myself."

"Then good luck to you. I admire a little hard-headedness in a man. Got a touch of it myself."

Dan excused himself and headed for the bunk house. Kearney and Jacob were already bedded down when he got there. Aaron was a few steps behind him.

"I think we ought to post a guard outside," Dan said. "Just in case . . ."

"Ash already told Simon to take the first watch," said the Irishman. "He's trying to get his brother to carry more responsibility around here."

Dan had misgivings about putting everyone's safety into Simon's hands. But then, he had to admit that Simon's eyesight was as good as anyone's, and he had a gun that would shoot and a voice that could holler. That, and alertness, was all a lookout needed.

"What is it that you're planning to do?" Jacob asked.

"I'm pulling out of here at daybreak. We need more manpower, so I'm riding over and talking to Barton about this. Then I'm heading for the Timberlake ranch, even though Ash thinks that talking to the captain is going to be a waste of time."

Kearney sat up on the edge of his bunk. He grinned, showing the space of a missing front tooth in the lamplight.

"By golly," he said, "I knew you were the best thing that ever happened to this place. Maybe we can get things turned around, now. If you can get Barton and Captain Timberlake to throw in with us, and maybe some of the smaller ranchers, we might just be able to get something done.''

In a way he was pleased that the others agreed with his plans, but in the back of his mind, he heard the sound of his father's voice. It was warning him.

"Never count on the strength of other men," it said. *"Build your own strength and rely on yourself."*

But what if your own strength wasn't enough? What if you were outmanned and outgunned? There was only one answer. You looked beyond yourself for allies. Otherwise you went down in defeat.

Dan crawled under the covers. It had been a tiring day, and he was still weak from losing blood. Sleep came quickly, and at dawn he was riding toward the Triple B.

It was a crisp fall morning, and here and there he could see patches of golden aspens. Up in the higher elevations, that same gold would be spilling down the mountainsides. To his way of thinking, this was a country to settle down in, and to grow old in. What finer legacy could a man leave to his sons and daughters? Freedom to be what you wanted, and justice for an unjust world, came to mind.

Over the years being cautious had become second nature to him. Instead of following the trail, he left it and rode roughly parallel to it. It was harder going, but he would be out of sight in case any of Keaton's men were watching.

All by himself, again, in the Arizona wilderness, he felt a sense of freedom that was tinged with only a little loneliness. He was frankly enjoying his own company, when he looked up and noticed the flight of a hawk. The graceful predator swooped low over a spill of rocks that lay up ahead, only closer to the trail. It seemed to be looking something, or someone, over. Then it soared on an air current that took it away from the rocky tumble that formed a sizable hill.

Dan halted, wondering what had attracted the bird's attention. He strained his eyes to see while he groped for the field glasses at the same time. Before he could retrieve the glasses from his saddlebag, he saw a flash of reflected light. He had no doubt that it was the reflection of the sun off a gun barrel. Someone was stationed in those rocks, waiting for him to ride down the trail. Dan figured that Keaton's man had watched him leave the ranch, and had come back to this spot for an ambush. It had been a good choice, for his would-be killer was sheltered by a veritable fortress. It would be difficult, if not impossible, to flush him out. He was thankful, both for his caution in not following the trail, and for the hawk's warning. Otherwise, he'd be riding into a death trap right now. Maybe the man up there was Keaton himself, although Dan doubted it. From what he'd heard of the rustler, he'd be more likely to hire someone to do the job. Then, too, it might be Draper who was waiting for him. At this point, Dan reckoned that it really didn't matter who it was.

Chapter Six

As quietly as possible, Dan made his way through the trees. He was thankful that his father had taught him to always do the unexpected.

"It gives a man the advantage if he's unpredictable," August Newland had said one morning when he himself had just acted in an unexpected way. "One day, in fact, it could save your life."

This was one of his father's lessons that he'd learned in spite of himself, and this was one more time when the learning had paid off.

It was clear that what he'd have to do was circle around those boulders and come up on the blind side of his would-be killer. Overhead, the hawk returned to make yet another pass above the human intruder.

Without warning, a ringtail scrambled to escape the footfall of the dun. He'd accidentally flushed it out of its hiding place. Dan tensed, concerned that the noise had alerted the bushwhacker. But after a moment of listening, he heard no response.

When he was a short distance past the rock spill, he dismounted and hobbled the horse. Then he darted across the small open area to the base. Making as little noise as possible, he began to climb. Soon he was having to pull himself upward, first over one boulder, and then another. His muscles strained, and he began to sweat.

He reached a spot where he was forced to step out onto a narrow ledge. Carefully he placed his right foot on the wind-and-rain-polished rim. But when he shifted his weight, his foot slipped out from under him. He grabbed for a handhold and felt the flesh tear as it scraped a jagged rock. Somehow he was able to hang on while he regained his footing. During those few seconds, he'd stifled the impulse to cry out. Now he simply clung to the side as he waited for his breathing to return to normal. The ground was far beneath him, and had he fallen, he would have been killed. While he waited, he listened for any sign that the bushwhacker had heard his approach. There was no sound but the whisper of the wind, so he continued to inch his way upward. When he reached the top, he caught sight of Ben Draper on the other side. Draper was watching the trail from the Lazy Q, his rifle in hand.

Dan saw that he couldn't get closer without warning the gunman. Still, from his present position, he had a chance. With his Colt ready, he called out.

"Are you waiting for somebody, Draper?"

There was a shower of dislodged stones as his enemy wheeled around at the sound of his voice. Draper fired blindly and ducked down.

Dan could see part of his green shirt, and this was the target at which he aimed. The bullet ricocheted off stone, creating flying splinters of rock. The splinters alone could do a lot of damage to a man's body. After that shot, Draper's gun was silent. Dan wondered if maybe he'd scored a lucky hit. He considered moving closer. Then he heard Draper scrambling down the far side.

He made his way down to the place where Draper had been waiting for him. There, he called out his name.

He got no answer, but he glimpsed the green shirt moving away from the spill. Draper was running fast and zigzagging through the trees. Dan couldn't get a clear shot, and he didn't relish shooting a man in the back anyway. Not even a bushwhacker.

That brought another question to mind. When did Draper start shooting from ambush? That wasn't his style. In the past, he always provoked a face-to-face shoot-out in front of witnesses. Why the change?

He climbed back down to the base, favoring his injured hand. Then he reclaimed the dun. He believed that it was more important than ever for him to talk with the ranchers and get their cooperation.

When he arrived at the Barton ranch, he noticed that it was well kept. It showed a woman's touch. As he rode up, he was greeted by a tall, raw-boned fellow with sunburned skin and sun-bleached hair.

Dan dismounted and offered his uninjured hand.

"Name's Dan Newland. I'm Ash Quigley's new foreman."

The man he'd assumed was Barton grinned and took his proffered hand.

"Glad to hear the Lazy Q has finally got a foreman. I'm Ames Barton. Come on in and meet the family. Looks like you need to get that hand bandaged.''

Dan liked him.

''I'd be pleased,'' he said. ''I rode over to let you know that we've come across maybe thirty head of cattle with your brand stamped on 'em. Expect you'll be wanting to fetch 'em back.''

A look of astonishment spread across the rancher's face.

''I surely do. The way we've been losing our steers is starting to hurt. Where in the world did you find them?''

''Over on Keaton's place. He had 'em hid in a little valley, waiting to change the brands. We had to argue with a couple of his men before they agreed to let 'em go, though.''

Barton rubbed his jaw.

''Somehow, I'm not real surprised. Did anyone get hurt?''

''On our side there was just Ash and me. I got a scratch, but I'm fine. Tony Quigley got there after it was over, and she helped drive the herd back to home turf.''

Barton chuckled at the mention of Tony.

''That there is quite a young woman, and I don't think anything she'd do would surprise me.''

Dan saw that two towheaded boys were peering out the window of the house. They were obviously curious about the stranger who was talking to their father.

''Come on in,'' invited the rancher. ''Mrs. Barton was about to fix a meal, and I expect you're hungry after that long ride.''

"Thanks," Dan said. "That is, if it's no trouble. I think I can do the lady's cooking justice."

Rowena Barton turned out to be plump and pretty. The air all around her smelled like spices, and she seemed pleased to have a visitor. He hadn't thought about it much before, but it occurred to him that it must be lonesome for a woman out here, with the ranches so far apart. Especially since getting from one to another was such risky business.

She gently bandaged his hand and then went about the business of cooking.

One thing was for sure, she spread a mighty fine table. There was roast meat on a platter, along with greens and slabs of fresh bread. And to top it off, there was apple cobbler made from dried fruit. He dug in with a hearty appetite, as did the entire Barton family.

He judged that the older boy was somewhere around ten, and figured his brother was seven or eight. They both listened eagerly, but they were well mannered and quiet, speaking only when spoken to.

"I'd have thought some of Captain Timberlake's herd would have been mixed in with the others," Barton said. "His ranch is one of the closer ones to the Circle K. Except for us and the Quigleys', it's one of the easiest for Keaton's outfit to hit."

"I've met the captain," Mrs. Barton said. "Just looking at him, one would judge him to be a formidable enemy. He has the military bearing of an officer."

Dan noticed that her husband made no comment, yet he had the feeling that Barton was keeping something to himself.

"I was planning on riding over and having a little talk with him," Dan said. "Do you think there's any chance that he'll join us against the rustlers?"

Barton lowered his fork and looked thoughtful.

"The man might surprise me," he said, "but I can't see him taking on the Circle K because they're rustling other ranchers' cattle. The captain believes in minding his own business, and he does it with concentration."

So Barton had made the same estimate as Ash. His prospects weren't bright. Still . . .

"I figured that it wouldn't hurt to ride over and have a talk with him."

"It's your own time, so why not? I'll send some of the boys over to your place, as soon as I can, to drive the cattle back. I'll send a couple of extras to stay awhile in case Ash has need of them."

Barton was turning out to be a worthwhile ally.

"Thanks. Those extra men would ease my mind considerably."

"Can I go too, Pa?" asked the older son with eagerness in his voice.

Barton reached over and tousled his blond hair affectionately.

"Not this time, Harvey. You've got to stay here and help your ma."

Harvey's face was a portrait of disappointment, but he didn't argue.

"Tell your men to keep a sharp lookout," Dan warned his host. "There was a fellow waiting to ambush me on my way over here. I was lucky and saw him first, and he took out in the direction of the

Circle K. Expect he's long gone, but that don't mean he might not be back, maybe with reinforcements."

Rowena Barton sighed.

"The lawlessness that goes on around here simply doesn't stop. Sometimes I wish that we'd stayed in Kentucky."

"Now, Row," soothed her husband as he reached out and touched her hand. "You don't mean that."

Dan looked away, embarrassed by the intimate moment.

"I'm afraid I do, Ames," she said with a tremor in her voice. "Trying to live in this place wears on a person's nerves after a while."

"It'll be different someday," Dan said. "I heard that General Crook and his troops are going to move against the Apache raiders that are holed up in the mountains. That will put an end to a lot of our troubles."

"That's all well and good," she said. "Now, if somebody could only do something about that den of thieves we have for neighbors."

"Well, ma'am, I guess that's going to be pretty much up to us."

She glanced across at her husband, knowing that he was going to be among the ones who made a stand against Keaton. Dan felt sorry that a family man like Barton had to be involved. However, Barton appeared to be a man of nerve and ability, one who would go the distance.

"When you need me, just send word," Barton said. "I'll be there with all the men I can gather."

"Appreciate it," Dan said. "We'll let you know."

As soon as he finished eating, he thanked the family for their hospitality. Then he went outside, accompanied by the rancher and his boy, Harvey. He climbed into the saddle of the dun, and with a wave of his hand, he rode off.

He'd heard some opinions about Captain Timberlake. Now he was going to find out for himself what the man was like. The big TL spread lay to the west of the Bartons' place, with part of its northern edge touching the Circle K. Dan took care to watch his back trail. Twice, he changed his direction briefly. Always, he did the unexpected, for Keaton would try to discourage any alliance of the ranchers against him. It was dusk when he first caught a glimpse of the sprawling log structure that the former Confederate officer had built for his home.

He was approaching the house when an armed man stepped from the shadows.

"Up with your hands, mister," he ordered.

He was holding a .45 and it was aimed at Dan's chest. Dan raised his hands.

"Who are you, and what are you doing here?" the guard demanded to know.

"Name's Dan Newland. I'm the foreman of the Lazy Q, and I'm here to see Captain Timberlake on a matter of mutual interest."

"Hey, Stringbean!" the guard called, taking care to keep his gun leveled on Dan.

A skinny half-grown kid came running.

"Go tell the captain that we've company. Tell him that he claims to be Ash Quigley's foreman, and that he's here on a matter of 'mutual interest.'"

The kid ran to the house. After a few minutes, he returned.

"Barnabas, the captain said to escort him inside."

Dan dismounted and submitted to a search. Barnabas relieved him of his pistol, as well as the hunting knife that he'd stuck inside his boot.

"This way," Barnabas ordered when he was satisfied that Dan was disarmed. "You can have 'em back when—and if—you leave."

Thus far, Dan wasn't impressed with Timberlake's neighborliness.

Stringbean led the way while Dan followed. Barnabas brought up the rear. Once inside the richly furnished house, he was ushered directly into the captain's presence.

The former Confederate officer stood behind a desk that took up the center of the book-lined room. His study had the fragrant smell of leather bindings and beeswax. The captain, however, wasn't as impressive as his surroundings. He was a man of medium height, clean shaven, and with a shock of sandy hair falling over his forehead. Dan judged him to be in his late thirties. He'd retained his military bearing, and he had a stern expression on his face.

"Captain, I believe you've been informed that I'm Dan Newland, foreman of the Lazy Q. My purpose in calling on you concerns the rustling that's been going on. We've discovered that Noah Keaton is responsible, and I'm trying to organize the ranchers to oppose this criminal activity."

Timberlake scarcely lifted an eyebrow.

"Sit down," he invited.

Pretending not to see Dan's outstretched hand,

Timberlake indicated a hide-covered arm chair near the desk that faced his own.

"May I offer you something to drink?" he asked.

"Whatever's handy," Dan said, confused by the man's behavior.

He went to a sideboard and poured whiskey into two glasses. He offered one to his unexpected guest.

"Now, what's this about Keaton?" he asked when he was seated.

"Well, first he roughed up one of our cowhands. Then he took three of our men by force and held them prisoner until we were able to get them loose— also by force. They'd gotten too close to a herd of cattle that wore the wrong brands. Ash Quigley and I finally found them in one of Keaton's hideaway meadows. Not a single one of more than sixty animals belonged to Keaton."

Timberlake took a drink and looked thoughtful.

"I must assume that they all belonged to Mr. Quigley."

Dan was getting his fill of the man's smugness.

"Only part of 'em. About half belonged to Ames Barton."

Timberlake set his glass down carefully, as if it were made of crystal, which it probably was.

"And how many head bore the TL brand?"

Dan could see it coming. His excuse for avoiding involvement.

"None. At least not this time."

Timberlake's face was a picture of complacence. There would be no help from him.

"And perhaps never," he said. "At any rate, I've no intention of risking my men, or my resources in an effort to defend someone else's property. Your cattle are your own responsibility, not mine.''

Dan finished the whiskey and set the glass on the desk.

"That's your choice, but a man like Keaton isn't going to leave you alone forever.''

Timberlake leaned back in his chair.

"Did you serve in the war?'' he asked.

"Yes. The Sixth Texas Cavalry. I had the rank of first lieutenant.''

"I see. Well, Lieutenant, I fought in that flame-and-smoke purgatory they call the Wilderness, and afterward at Spotsylvania. The battle at Spotsylvania cost 18,000 lives on both sides, and that's where General Stuart was mortally wounded. There are still nights when I can smell death all around me, and I can hear the screams of the wounded and dying. I wake up choking, as if trying to catch my breath in the thick, acrid smoke of battle. My heart is pounding so hard that I fear it will break through my flesh. No sir. I've had my fill of battle. Enough to last an eternity. In this conflict, you will have to fight without me, although I wish you and your neighbors the victory, for I despise a thief.''

Dan got up from his chair and looked Timberlake in the eye.

"I believe there's nothing more to be said, then. Thanks for the drink.''

The captain nodded and called for his servant.

A dignified man, in his later years, entered the room. He was wearing a dark jacket and a string tie.

"Lucas, please show Mr. Newland to the door, and have Barnabas escort him off the property.''

"Yes, sir," was Lucas's reply.

Barnabas was waiting outside the door.

"Here's your sidearm," he said, returning the Colt. "And your knife."

Dan mounted the dun, and Barnabas rode beside him for about a mile. Then he stopped.

"You can go on by yourself now, Newland."

"Fine. You can tell your boss that he's gotten rid of me, but he hasn't gotten rid of the trouble that's setting on his northern boundary. One of these days, he's going to have to get off that chair of his and leave his fancy library. He's going to have to fight for his property or else lose it. That's not a guess. That's a fact."

"I reckon when the boss wants your opinion, he'll ask for it."

With that, Barnabas turned and retraced the path they'd taken.

Dan continued on in the moonlight. He was suddenly anxious to be off Timberlake range and back on Barton land. The war had wounded the captain in a way that had never healed. A soldier could ofttimes survive the insult of a bullet wound or a bayonet slash and still be a man. But Timberlake's nerve and dignity had been destroyed, and in a real sense, his manhood. He'd surrounded himself with the trappings of a strong, successful pioneer, and they appeared to be holding Keaton back for the present. But the illusion was flimsy, and it wouldn't be able to withstand the slightest aggression. The figure in that book-lined room was a pitiful imitation of what Captain Timberlake must have been. As soon as

Keaton got a hint of that, he'd be quick to exploit the weakness.

But Dan still had problems of his own. There was the rest of the stolen cattle to find. There was a ranch to defend. And somewhere along the way, he was going to have to deal with Draper.

He was tired, for it had been a long day, and night riding was more difficult. When he came to a stand of trees, he stopped and made a shelter of the branches. Then he spread his bedroll on a cushion of fragrant needles and slept until dawn.

He awoke hungry, for it had been a long time since he'd sat at Rowena Barton's table. But this close to the southern border of the Circle K, he didn't want to risk a fire. He simply ignored the complaints of his stomach.

There was no need for him to ride to the Barton place, for he'd only be telling Ames Barton what he already knew about his neighbor. Ash wouldn't be surprised either.

As it turned out, he hadn't gone far, when Barton rode down from a hill where he'd been watching.

"Thought you'd be coming back about now," said the rancher.

Dan shrugged. "I had to try," he said.

"No harm in that. Besides, you had to see for yourself. The captain struts around and acts like he's got a lot of starch, but the war took all that away."

"For his sake, I hope Keaton never finds out."

"Yeah. You've got to feel sorry for him. But that means that the rest of us are on our own. He's not about to offer any help."

"I suppose that getting a federal marshal out here is too much to expect."

"It's just not going to happen," Barton said. "Nor federal troops, either. We're going to have to take care of this ourselves."

It was a story he'd heard before. With few exceptions, the people of Arizona Territory were pretty much on their own.

"Well, I've got to get back," Dan said. "We're shorthanded as it is, and I worry about Tony, not to mention those two old men."

"She sure has turned into a pretty young woman. It's a shame that Ash's plan to send her back east didn't work out."

It seemed to him that everybody in the Territory knew about Ash's attempt to give his granddaughter a new kind of life. Only Tony didn't appear to have any regrets. Maybe she already had the kind of life she wanted right here in Arizona, even with all the dangers and lack of social graces.

"Actually, I happened across their wagon when I was coming this way from Fort Yuma. At the time, I wondered why they were out there alone. But since we were newly acquainted, I didn't want to ask."

"He's real fond of that girl," Barton said, "and sometimes his feelings get in the way of his good judgment."

"Expect you're right. Appreciate your help, Barton. Be careful."

"You too."

Dan headed straight for the Lazy Q, hoping that nothing had happened in his absence. Somehow, he felt that Keaton would check on his men first, and bide his time before launching an attack.

When he reached the rock spill where Draper had laid in wait for him, he gave it a wide berth. He didn't believe the old saying that lightning never strikes twice in the same place. He knew different. Lightning strikes anywhere it pleases.

Ash was watching for him when he neared the ranch. He was eager for news.

"Barton's with us on this," Dan said.

The old man looked relieved.

"I was counting on him. Barton is a good man. Did you see the captain like you was plannin' to?"

Dan figured he already had a good idea about what had happened.

"Yeah," he said. "I did."

"It was a waste of time, wasn't it."

It wasn't a question that Ash had asked, it was a statement.

"Not quite. I needed to know, for sure, whether or not I could count on him. I found that he had the worst kind of war injury a man can have. His nerve was amputated."

"A good way to put it. I sized him up as being a lot of strutting and no guts."

Dan led his mount into the stable and began to strip it of saddle and bridle. Ash followed him inside.

"Did you have any trouble whilst you was gone?"

"Some. Draper tried to ambush me on the way to the Triple B. It's plain that he didn't succeed, but he got away. Didn't expect him to try something like that. I thought he'd want to meet me face-to-face.''

"What made him change his style, do you reckon?''

"Don't know. Keaton and a whole lot of money, I suppose.''

"Ever since I got back from Yuma, I've been feelin' edgy, like something is about to happen,'' Ash said.

Dan forked some hay into the manger.

"I guess that waiting for something to happen can be almost as bad as when it finally does.''

Ash moved in closer and squinted at his face in the dim light.

"Something's bothering you, son, I can tell it.''

Dan busied himself rubbing down the dun.

"I learned something today that wasn't too pleasant. I learned that there's worse things that can happen to a man than dying. Losing your nerve and being afraid to defend yourself is about the worst there is.''

"I'll throw in with you there.''

"Barton is sending some men over to help. I thought I'd ride out again and see what I can do to be worrisome.''

"If you're set on doing it, I guess I don't have to tell you to be careful.''

Ash was right. He didn't.

Chapter Seven

Ever since the ugly scene at the main house, Emma tried to keep busy with chores elsewhere. When she had to fix meals there, she did her work as quickly and quietly as possible. Then she retreated to her own cabin. She'd tried to make Noah Keaton care for her, to find her indispensable if not attractive. Now, she wondered if that had even been possible. She doubted that he'd ever found anyone indispensable.

The soggy shirt she hoisted to the clothesline dripped water down her arm. She was pinning it in place when she saw Keaton leaving the house. Without so much as a glance in her direction, he swaggered toward the stable. From her place of concealment behind the line of laundry, Emma watched him go inside.

"And what is Himself up to now?" she wondered out loud, when after a few minutes he emerged from the stable and went back to the house.

Before she could finish hanging the rest of the wet

laundry, Felix Collins came out of that same stable, leading his horse. He mounted and rode east.

Emma felt a sense of uneasiness. Felix had been a good friend to her late husband, Lester, and Keaton was blaming Felix for all the things that had been going wrong. She'd seen the look of rage on Keaton's face when he'd learned of the deaths of Rumfelt and McLaren, and that the herd had been lost.

In her opinion, things had gone too far with the capture of Ash Quigley's men. Keaton wasn't satisfied with teaching them a lesson. He was angry with Felix for not ordering them killed. With what had happened since, she had no doubt that Felix was in danger. In his place, she'd have sneaked off in the night and ridden as far and as fast as a horse would take her.

What are you talking about? she said to herself. *You are in his place.*

This was the first time she'd let it sink in. Keaton had no conscience, and Emma knew too much about his business.

Emma dumped the washtub with one strong heave and shoved it back into place in the wash shack. On her way to the cabin, she saw the new fellow, Draper, ride out in the same direction as Felix. What had been uneasiness became fear.

Inside the cabin, she glanced around. Her possessions were pitifully few. Wasting no time, she slipped off her calico and pulled on a pair of Lester's old pants. She tightened them around her middle with a worn leather belt. Next, she put on a faded shirt, letting the tail hang loose. A floppy hat completed her outfit.

She grabbed a burlap bag and went around the room, gathering her things into it like she was harvesting berries. Lester's old hogleg was the last thing that she took, after first loading it.

She paused at the door and glanced toward Keaton's house. It would be hours before she was expected there. For the time being, he'd be occupied with his books and accounts. She was about to step outside the cabin, when she was proved wrong.

Keaton appeared in the doorway as one of the stable hands walked toward him leading his favorite horse.

"The sorrel's ready, Mr. Keaton," he called.

She watched as Keaton took the reins and mounted his latest acquisition. To her, he looked awkward, and totally unworthy of such a fine animal. When he too headed east, any doubts Emma had clung to disappeared.

The minute he was out of sight, she ducked through the lines of bouncing clothes and headed for the corral. The way she was dressed, she looked like a cowhand, and no one was apt to recognize her. She passed by a man who was repairing a harness, and was relieved that he paid her no mind.

Emma saddled a sturdy-looking dapple gray, and with only the contents of a burlap bag to compensate for a lifetime of work, she rode off. Not once did she look back.

There was little hope that she could parallel the route that Keaton and the others had taken and reach Felix in time to warn him. But she had to try. Felix and Lester had ridden the trail together, but more than that, Felix had always treated her with respect.

In a lot of ways he was more of a man than Keaton could ever be.

The country they were headed for was a likely place for a man to meet with an accident—or to simply disappear. She pushed the gray hard until she caught sight of Keaton. He was some distance to her left, but they were almost even, He seemed to be taking his time. She figured that Draper was to be the executioner, and he was simply coming along to check on the job.

Fighting despair, she kicked the gray in the sides to urge it on. Trees, brush, and rocks stood between their parallel journeys. She wasn't worried about being seen, especially since they wouldn't be watching for her. None of the three were in any particular hurry, so she managed to get close to Felix and Draper. She heard them before she caught a glimpse of the gunman.

"Hey, Collins, wait up!" Draper shouted.

She turned the gray to her left, trying to close the space between herself and Draper's voice. The hogleg was out, ready for use.

Felix had turned to face his executioner. She couldn't hear what he said, but she could see them both clearly, now. Draper had his gun out, and Felix didn't stand a chance.

The gray was moving fast, and there was no way that Emma could take careful aim. She simply threw up the hogleg and fired. Draper flung himself off his horse and slid into the brush. She fired blindly after him, desperately hoping for a hit. Felix was riding toward her instead of turning on Draper.

"No!" she yelled.

But her warning was too late. There was the sound of another gunshot, and Felix fell to the ground. Blood stained the back of his shirt. From the corner of her eye, she saw Keaton in the distance. He was just sitting there on his fancy horse taking everything in like it was some kind of show. Disgust and alarm fought for first place in her consciousness. She had to get away from there.

They both had good mounts, and there was no chance that she could outrun them on the gray. What she had to do was find a place where she could make a stand. With no help and only a small supply of ammunition, she knew she couldn't hold out for long. She needed a miracle, but there had been no miracles in Emma Huffman's life.

The gray needed little urging to run from the noise, the smoke, and the death smell. She headed it west, the opposite direction from the Circle K. It was her only chance, and maybe if she got far enough, she might run into some of Ash Quigley's people.

She dared not look back, but she knew they were close behind. There was gunfire. They were closer than she thought. Time was running out.

Just ahead, there was a dip in the landscape. Nothing else looked promising. A large, dead tree trunk that had been felled by the wind lay at the top edge. As soon as she reached it, she dived for cover behind the trunk. She aimed her sidearm and prepared to defend herself. Draper and Keaton pulled up.

"He's behind that wood," she heard Draper say.

"Then get him!" came the order.

Both killers began shooting into the branches of

her cover. Splinters flew everywhere. In desperation she fired Lester's gun, with the thought that she'd likely be seeing him again soon. Somehow, she managed to get Draper in her sights and fired a second time. She thought she'd grazed him, but he stayed in the saddle. Now the two of them loosed what amounted to a bombardment. She huddled against the side of the hollow, aware that the end was near. The tree that shielded her was being shot into small pieces, and she wouldn't have time to reload once her gun was empty.

When she'd given up any hope of survival, she heard a gunshot from behind her. A shower of dirt sprayed up in front of the sorrel, causing it to rear back, nearly unseating Keaton. Other shots followed from the same source. While she watched in wonderment, Draper turned tail and ran with Keaton hot on his heels.

Emma looked up to find out who her rescuer was, and saw a young man riding down the slope on a dun. She noticed that he was muscular with strong-looking features that were framed by a dark beard. Despite the terror she'd just experienced, she found herself wishing she was a dozen years younger.

"Thanks," she called out. "You couldn't have showed up at a better time."

He appeared startled to hear a woman's voice, causing her to remember that she didn't look anything like a woman.

He rode up to where she was now standing.

"Are you all right, ma'am?" he inquired.

"I am now. Those two sidewinders that you just ran off killed a friend of mine a little while ago."

He dismounted and helped her from her shredded fortress.

"They sure made a mess of this," he said. "One of those men looked to me like Ben Draper."

"He was," Emma said. "Is he a friend of yours?"

"An old enemy. I'd risk a guess that the fellow with him was Noah Keaton."

"That makes twice you're right."

He climbed into the saddle and reached down to help her up behind him.

"What was your friend's name?" he asked. "The one that was killed."

"Felix Collins, Keaton's foreman."

"I've heard of him. I'm Ash Quigley's foreman, Dan Newland."

"I've heard of you, as well. One of the reasons that Felix was killed was because he refused to shoot your three men, or to order them shot. I used to be Keaton's housekeeper. My name's Emma Huffman."

She wasn't sure how he'd react to that information. But it didn't seem to make a difference.

"I reckon I'd better take you to the Quigley place for a while. I'm sure my boss will be glad to have you stay as long as you need to."

"Thanks," she said. "I used to know Asher Quigley real well, and I think I'd like to renew the acquaintance."

They hadn't ridden far when they came upon the gray. Dan helped her into the saddle, which shouldn't have surprised her, but it was the kind of treatment she wasn't accustomed to receiving.

"I may not be doing you a favor by taking you to the ranch," he said after they'd traveled some distance. "It's just that I don't know what else to do with you."

He didn't have to explain.

"Keaton's mad. That's for sure. He's been used to having things his own way. Of late, I've begun to think that he's a little bit crazy. Ever since he found out about that cattle you took back, he's been fury on legs. Now that he's gotten rid of Felix, I expect he'll turn his attention to Asher's place. I can shoot, and I'd be pleased to throw in with you."

She was surprised to see him look at her with an expression of respect. It was a good feeling.

When they got to the ranch, she was pleased to see Asher come out to meet them.

"Well I'll be. It's Emma Huffman, as I live and breathe."

"It's good to see you, Asher. Got room for a homeless neighbor?"

"I've always got room for you, Emma. Get down and come on inside."

His welcome made her feel good, and she realized that despite the way Felix had died, and the fact that his killers were running loose, she was feeling better than she had in a long, long time. Being treated with respect was rekindling her own self-respect. She liked it.

Dan followed them into the cabin.

"Mrs. Huffman was having some difficulty," he said. "Keaton and Draper had her pinned down in a little hollow. They didn't intend to let her leave there alive."

She watched the expression on Asher's face change from pleasure to disgust.

"Did you get 'em?" he asked.

"I just persuaded them to leave. Mrs. Huffman managed to wound Draper."

"Only nicked him a little," she said. "He killed Felix Collins on Keaton's orders. Poor Felix never had a chance. I tried to stop it, but I couldn't."

Asher took her arm and seated her at the table.

"You need to have a cup of hot tea while Dan takes care of the animals."

"That sounds real good, and I could use a bite to eat, if you have one."

"I think I can come up with some scrambled eggs and a biscuit or two."

"I'd be real thankful."

The door opened then, and Tony Quigley walked in. One look told her that the young woman didn't welcome her nearly as warmly as the others had done. Suddenly, Emma felt like an intruder from the enemy camp. And that, she thought, was exactly what she was.

"Step in here and say howdy to Mrs. Huffman," Ash instructed his granddaughter as she stood poised for flight.

"Howdy," she said. "Now, if you'll excuse me, I've got chores to do."

Before Emma could reply, she backed out the doorway and disappeared.

"You've got to overlook Tony's behavior. She ain't too strong on good manners yet."

Emma knew that manners weren't the problem here.

"Don't worry, Asher. I expect she was surprised to find somebody from the Circle K sitting at her table, that's all."

"It's kind of you to take it that way, Emma, but she disappointed me. Sometimes I just don't know what to do with her."

He scraped the eggs onto a plate and added a couple of biscuits. It had been so long since she'd eaten that they looked and smelled better than a meal she'd once enjoyed with Lester in a French restaurant in New Orleans.

"I expect this cookin' ain't near what you're used to," he apologized.

She looked up at his sympathetic face and smiled.

"It's just fine, Asher. It's been a long time since anybody saw to my comforts. And while I'm thinking about it, I like that young foreman of yours. He's a gentleman for sure."

Ash filled two teacups and sat down opposite. He pushed one of them toward her.

"I was real lucky to come across Dan's path. Tony sets great store by him, but she'd never own up to it. Especially not to him."

"A woman ought to keep a fellow guessing. That'll make her more interesting to him, don't you think?"

Her host grimaced.

"Ain't it just like a woman to say something like that."

"Well it's true, and your granddaughter probably knows these things by instinct."

She watched him stare into his teacup.

"It's the only way she could possibly know about

'woman things.' There sure hasn't been a woman around here to tell her.''

Emma could feel his regret, for it was tangible.

''This old world isn't the way it ought to be, is it, Asher?''

''No. It sure ain't.''

They shared the silence for a moment before she brought up what was on her mind.

''I'd like to stick around until Keaton and Draper are made to answer for the meanness they've been doing. I can cook and clean, and I can do other chores too.''

She watched his expression carefully.

''You know you're welcome, Emma, and we can use any help that you can give us.''

She felt a sense of relief and wondered why she was teary-eyed all of a sudden. Had she grown so accustomed to Keaton's abuse that she'd lost track of what it meant to be treated like a human being? She swallowed the lump in her throat and managed one word.

''Thanks.''

Sensing her mood, he got up and patted her shoulder.

''Don't worry about the way Tony's acting. She'll come around. I imagine that when she gets used to your being here, you'll be able to teach her a few things that she ought to know.''

Emma recalled the stormy look on the girl's face, and she wasn't able to share her friend's optimism. Before she could say anything, though, there was a shout from outside.

''Hello the house!''

"Must be the boys that Ames Barton promised to send over," Asher said. "I'd better go out and make 'em welcome."

That bit of news was good. She figured that if Barton was joining forces with the Lazy Q, then maybe they'd have a chance.

Chapter Eight

Dan came from the stable just in time to see Tony leave the house. She didn't look at all pleased about finding the Huffman woman installed in her home. He could understand the misgivings she must have, for under other circumstances he wouldn't have trusted Emma Huffman either. But she'd had the spunk to defy Keaton and try to save a friend. Because of that, she was out of a job and into serious trouble. To his surprise, Ash not only accepted her at face value, he actually seemed to like her.

Tony saw him and headed straight toward him. He got the feeling that he was in the path of a Texas tornado and there was no escaping its wrath.

"Why did you bring that woman here?" she demanded.

"I suppose you think I should have left her stranded out there in the wilderness, with two killers shooting at her."

She put her hands on her hips and stood so close to him that he could smell the musky scent of her skin and see the little crinkles at the corners of her eyes.

"She's one of them. Didn't you stop to think that the gun battle was staged just for you, so you'd feel obliged to haul her back here so she could keep an eye on us."

He suppressed the urge to laugh.

"Mrs. Huffman wasn't one of them," he reasoned. "She merely worked as Keaton's housekeeper."

Tony raised an eyebrow.

"Really?" she said. "I heard that she was more to him than 'merely' his housekeeper."

Dan could feel the heat flush his face. He didn't like to discuss such things with a woman, and she shouldn't have mentioned it.

"I don't waste my time listening to gossip," he told her in a voice that sounded prissy even to himself, "and you'd be a lot better off if you didn't, either."

She puffed up then like a mad bantam rooster, and he was glad that looks couldn't kill. Otherwise his time on earth would have been over.

"When I want to hear a sermon I'll find a preacher, not a know-it-all cattle nursemaid like yourself."

She made a move to step around him just as there was a shout. Startled, she paused.

"Who's that?"

He saw the two riders at the edge of the clearing.

"I believe it's Barton's riders that he was going to send over."

To the men he called, "Come on in!"

They rode up to where he and Tony were waiting. One was an older fellow with streaks of gray showing in his beard. He looked tough, lean, and experienced. The man beside him was a lot younger with a face that hadn't seen much of life's troubles. He had light-colored hair that he wore down to his shoulders, and he took care about how he dressed. They dismounted and introduced themselves.

"We're the ones that Mr. Barton sent over to lend you folks a hand," said the older man. "My name's George Flagg. My partner here is Matt Allander."

"Appreciate the help," Dan said as he shook hands.

"Glad we can give it. Mr. Barton sent some others on to drive his cattle home."

Tony, who was still standing at Dan's side, gave his arm a firm pinch.

"Oh, and this here is Miss Antonia Quigley," he said quickly. "She's the boss's granddaughter."

Flagg nodded politely in her direction, but Allander bowed slightly from the waist.

"I'm delighted to meet such a lovely lady," he said.

Dan noticed the pained look on Flagg's face at his partner's pretentiousness. He was pretty aggravated, himself, to see how Tony was eating up that hot air like it was gingerbread.

Ash and Emma came out to welcome the newcomers.

"You really are undermanned," Flagg said. "I expected at least a few more around here with things being the way they are."

"My brother and three others are close by," assured Ash, who seemed embarrassed to have the shortcoming pointed out. "They're keeping alert for any trouble while they're working."

Dan wondered what work could be more important than protecting Tony, the house, and the stock. When he'd ridden off and found Emma, he'd assumed the others would be guarding the place. Flagg had hit on a sore spot as far as he was concerned. Sometimes he just didn't understand Ash's reasoning at all. Part of the time he was sensible and cautious, and part of the time he was downright irresponsible and reckless.

"I think you should call them all in to help protect the ladies," Allander said. "Even though there are four of us, now, that might not be enough."

Dan halfway expected Tony to start ranting at Allander for calling her a lady, or for suggesting that she needed protection. To his surprise, she held her tongue. And even though he agreed with Allander, it irked him that he'd horned in and told Ash what to do.

Emma Huffman spoke up.

"I firmly believe that whatever Keaton is going to do, he's going to do it soon."

"How come you know so much about it?" asked Tony, who was ever suspicious of Emma.

"I've come to know Keaton and his ways," she replied. "He's been frustrated too many times of late. His business has been threatened and he's going to react. At times like this, a pressure builds inside of him. When he watched poor Felix being killed, that must have released some of the pressure, but not enough and not for long. Besides, he's probably discovered that I've left his place, and he's figured out that I'm the one who wounded Draper. That alone would probably set him off.''

Dan figured that Draper had gotten a good look at him during their exchange of gunfire, and Draper would assume that he'd taken Emma back to the Lazy Q. That would only prod him and Keaton harder to attack.

''When are Simon and the others coming in?'' he asked Ash.

''Before dark. About suppertime, I guess. I expect they'll follow their hunger toward the cooking pot.''

Dan hoped that wouldn't be too late.

''Grab your gear,'' he told Flagg and Allander. ''I'll show you to the bunkhouse.''

When they were out of Ash's hearing, Flagg voiced his doubts.

''Do you think Mr. Quigley realizes how serious this situation is, sending his men away like that?''

Dan shrugged and reached for the bunkhouse door.

''I don't know. I can't figure him out sometimes.''

He was remembering the dangerous trek to Fort Yuma that had ended in disappointment. At least it hadn't ended in death.

''Glad you're both here,'' he said, and he meant it, even though he hated to see that Tony had taken a shine to Allander.

Just before dark, Simon and the others came riding in just as Ash had predicted. Emma cooked a big meal for everyone, shooing Ash out of the house while she worked. Even Tony showed up for supper, thanks to her appetite and her new beau. All through the evening she behaved just like she'd spent her life in a boarding school. Dan couldn't see a thing wrong with her manners, and even her grandfather seemed pleasantly surprised.

As soon as the meal was over Aaron excused himself.

"Think I'll spend the night in my favorite tree," he said.

"Don't fall out," Tony warned.

Dan and the other hands were getting ready to head for the bunkhouse when Ash invited Emma to share Tony's sleeping quarters. He noticed that Tony got quiet as death. When Emma thanked Ash and started toward the calico curtains, Tony turned and walked out the door. In a way, he felt sorry for her. Her grandfather could be high-handed at times.

Dan fetched his bedroll and headed for the wood-pile. There were two tall stacks of logs and kindling on either side of a large, flat rock that was about waist high. The rock was handy for a nap in the sun between bouts of wood chopping. The L shape that the rock and the wood piles formed was a readymade shelter of sorts. From behind it, he had a good view of all the approaches to the clearing. Here he would have some protection from the wind, and it would be warmer during the night. He didn't envy Aaron his treetop perch.

For a time he just sat there with his back against the rock, looking at the sky. He'd discovered that many Arizona nights were clear, and this one was no exception. Kearney had agreed to take his place later on, and until then he was content to let the night inch away while he pondered on the mysteries of nature and the ways of men—and women.

An hour or more must have passed when he heard a footfall. His hand went instinctively to his firearm.

"Are you awake?" Tony asked softly.

"A man doesn't volunteer for guard duty in order to go to sleep," he retorted.

She was bundled against the chill of a fall night and hunkered down beside him.

"When are you going back to the house?" he asked, for he guessed that she was bedding down in the barn.

"Do you really trust that Huffman woman?" she asked instead of answering his question.

He knew he was on dangerous ground, and he picked his words with care.

"I think so. At least I trust that she's got good reason to despise her friend's killer."

"Well, she's got no right to waltz in here and take over my place like she owns it."

Dan found himself squirming mentally.

"I guess you'll have to take that up with your grandfather."

Now he felt Tony easing herself closer.

"A lot of good that will do. Grandpa is stuck on her. I wouldn't be a bit surprised if he takes it into his head to marry her."

Dan thought about that. The idea of Ash Quigley getting married to a woman who was twenty-five years younger struck his funny bone. He barely managed to turn the laugh into a cough, but it didn't fool her.

"You may think it's funny, but I don't. Grandpa is easy pickings for the likes of a woman like her."

"Maybe so," he said, "but I doubt if you're going to be able to tell Ash what to do with his life."

She struggled to her feet, tugging the blanket tighter around her shoulders.

"I'm afraid you're right this time. It's a shame that men don't have any sense."

She left so fast that he felt a wake of cold air from her departure.

But tonight Dan had more urgent worries than his boss's matrimonial intentions. He listened for any unusual sounds, and peered into the darkness. They'd been lucky so far, but he knew it was just the calm before the storm.

He lay back and listened to the *yip, yip* of a distant coyote, and figured that no sound on earth was lonesomer. After a while he changed his position, trying for one that held more comfort yet still allowed him to scan the woods that circled the clearing. The wind shifted briefly, and he imagined he smelled smoke. But there was no sign of its source, and he only smelled it for an instant. He decided that it had been his imagination.

Another hour passed by his reckoning, and Kearney came to take his place.

"It's colder than a banker's heart out here," complained the big Irishman. "Has Aaron fallen out of that tree yet?"

"I haven't heard any commotion. Guess he's still up there."

Dan had come to have a lot of respect for Aaron.

Kearney picked a spot for himself nearby and placed his rifle across his knees.

"Well, my friend, it appears we've had the luck of the Irish so far," he said.

"Maybe. But I thought I smelled smoke awhile ago. It could be that I was dreaming, but maybe not."

"Even a dream like that makes me plenty nervous."

"That's why I'm going on a little scouting expedition before it gets daylight. That is, if I can get my horse out of the stable without getting shot by an irate female."

Kearney chuckled.

"I thought Tony was goin' to bust her corset. She was sure put out about the Huffman woman staying in her quarters."

Dan didn't know a whole lot about female undergarments, but he doubted if Tony ever had a close association with anything as constraining as a corset.

"I'm going to try to get back here by daylight," he said. "But if there's anyone out there, I want to know where they are."

"Guess you know to be careful."

"Don't worry yourself, Kearney. I plan to do that too."

When Dan got to the barn, he paused before going inside.

"It's okay, it's me," he called softly. If there was anything he didn't want to do, it was to alarm Tony. That was apt to get him a bullet hole in his shirt.

He waited a few seconds but heard no answer, so he pushed the door open. There was just enough light inside for him to see her shadowy outline curled up in a corner. Her breathing was deep and rhythmic. He went over to one of the stalls.

The dun recognized him and nuzzled his hand. Dan saddled it and led it outside, where he mounted and rode in the direction the whiff of smoke had come from.

At times the moonlight was blocked, and he had to ride with greater care. Once he lost his way in the thick woods. It was nearly dawn when he heard the sound of muffled voices. He pulled his rifle from the scabbard and stopped to listen. The voices were coming from an encampment in a nearby hollow. Silently Dan eased forward. The campfire had burned down until it was nothing more than glowing embers. He counted eleven outlaws all together. Keaton wasn't taking any chances.

"Quit wasting time," growled a heavyset man who was probably Keaton.

It looked like the expected attack was about to happen. Dan saw that Draper was with them too. His shirt was torn, and there was a bandage on one arm where Emma had shot him.

Keaton issued another order, and eleven outlaws rode single file from the hollow. To Dan they seemed to float like evil specters as they wended their way among the trees. The scene was eerie, and he was filled with apprehension, knowing their purpose and destination.

He followed as closely as he dared. It galled him that there was nothing he could do against so many, and his only hope was to somehow warn the ranch.

When they were getting close to the Lazy Q, Keaton ordered his men to halt. While Dan watched, they fanned out and advanced in the new formation. He knew that he would have to act soon, but for a while longer he'd follow along and wait.

Chapter Nine

With his hat pulled low on his head, Dan worked his way to the far left edge of the advancing line and moved forward as if he were one of them. When they were only minutes away from a surprise attack, he drew his revolver and fired two quick warning shots. Then he slid from his horse and dropped to his knees. That ought to wake up the ranch, he thought. The response on both sides was immediate.

The outlaws were caught off guard, and gunfire from the ranch sent them all diving for cover.

"I'll have the hide of the man who fired those first shots," yelled Keaton, thinking that one of his own had done it.

Through the acrid smoke and dim light, Dan couldn't see very well, but he could tell that Kearney, Aaron, and the others were holding the outlaws off. He hoped that Tony would stay in the barn, but that was something he couldn't count on. She always found a way to be in the middle of whatever was going on.

The instant that Dan left the saddle, the dun ran

away, leaving him to work his way forward as best he could. He was in danger from both sides. He was still on his knees, crawling around the perimeter, when one of Keaton's men spotted him and recognized that he wasn't one of theirs.

''Over there!'' he yelled and fired.

Dan rolled to his left as a bullet hit the spot where he'd been just a second before. Dan returned the fire, and the outlaw fell backward. He was either dead or wounded.

''Hey! One of 'em's crawling around over there,'' came another shout from the woods. ''He shot Louie.''

''Get him!'' Keaton yelled.

Now that he'd been recognized, they were going to try to pin him down. Dan knew that he had to make a run for it. He leaped into the clearing and sprinted across it, praying that Kearney and the others would look before they shot. His steps were followed by a rain of bullets from the woods. The ones at the bunkhouse and at the wood stacks started laying down cover fire to take the pressure off Dan. He raced for the stacks and slid bellydown across the flat rock, landing at Kearney's feet.

''Welcome home,'' said the Irishman with a lopsided grin. ''Glad to see that you made it back okay.''

Dan turned and emptied his revolver into the enemy line.

From the corner of his eye, he saw that one of Keaton's men had succeeded in getting close to the house. A torch of light blazed up, and the outlaw tossed it onto the roof. Kearney saw it too, and cried out in alarm.

"Fire!"

Dan hoped that the roof was damp enough to discourage the flames, but it turned out not to matter, for the torch rolled down the sloping roof and dropped to the ground before it could ignite the wood. The dead grass around it blazed up, though, presenting another danger. The outlaws kept up a steady stream of gunfire to insure that no one could get close enough to douse the flames.

"The house is going to burn!" came a shout from the edge of the bunkhouse. It was Allander.

Dan felt a bitterness in his throat for what they were attempting, as well as alarm for the ones who were inside. He dared not let himself think that Tony might be in there too. He knew what had to be done, and some things were best done without too much deliberation.

"Cover me!" he ordered.

He ran for the house. Ash saw him coming and had the door open. Dan threw himself inside. One glance told him that Tony wasn't there. Simon was trying to help Emma, who was choking on the smoke that was pouring into the house from the burning grass.

"You've got to get out," he said.

"We'd like that a whole lot, but they'll shoot us if we try to leave," Simon said.

"Would you rather stay here while the place burns down around you?" he demanded. "Kearney and the others are keeping 'em busy. Come on, we've got a chance."

Emma coughed, again, the effort bending her almost double, and Ash was having trouble getting his breath. Dan grabbed the woman around her waist, and, keeping his body between her and the outlaws, he ran with her, half dragging her toward Kearney's woodpile fortress. He couldn't tell if Ash and Simon were following.

When he reached the wooden stacks, he shoved Emma to the ground where she was shielded by the rock. He looked back toward the house. Ash was almost to safety, but Simon had stayed by the house, beating the flames with his coat. He'd made himself an easy target, and only the thick smoke had saved him thus far. Aaron, Flagg, and the others were trying to draw the enemy fire away from the old man.

"No, Simon, let it go!" Ash shouted when he turned and saw what his brother was trying to do. But Simon appeared not to hear him and continued fighting the flames like they were demons.

Ash shrugged out of his own jacket and started to run back and help him, but the big Irishman grabbed his boss and held him fast.

Dan grabbed Ash's jacket and went in his place. He'd almost reached him when Simon took a bullet and went down. Taking his place, Dan pounded out the last of the burning grass with the borrowed coat. He didn't intend that Simon Quigley be wounded or die in vain. With the fire out, the smoke was dissipating, making him an even better target. He grasped Simon under his arms and dragged him back to where the others had taken refuge. While the wounded man was being cared for, Dan lay gasping for breath with oxygen-deprived lungs.

Suddenly he became aware that the gun battle had ceased. There was only an occasional shot from a great distance. The enemy was retreating. Dan pushed himself to a sitting position and looked around.

Emma and Ash were frantically attending Simon's wounds. While Dan watched, Emma got to her feet. With a sigh of regret, she drew her arm across her soot-stained face, and he knew that Simon was dead.

"This should never have happened," Ash said in a voice cracked with emotion. "Simon was the gentle one. He didn't deserve to be hurt."

"None of us did," Emma said gently.

The others were leaving their posts since the firing had stopped. Tony came running from the barn, her long hair flying out behind her.

"What happened to Uncle Simon?" she cried.

When she saw his lifeless body on the ground, she made a choking sound.

"He was shot while saving the house from burning down," Ash said. The words came out as if they were sticking in his throat.

Tony put her arm around her grandfather and knelt with him beside the fallen man. Dan and the others backed away in respect for their loss.

"He really did save the house," Ash repeated.

Dan noticed that Flagg, who was standing some distance away from the others, was motioning to him. Dan went over to find out what he wanted.

"I was just out there," he said, nodding toward the woods, "and I counted three dead. It's too bad that Keaton wasn't one of 'em. That old cow thief is probably madder than a hornet right about now, and I'm wondering what he's going to do next.''

Whatever it was, there were three less outlaws to worry about.

''Your guess is as good as mine about that,'' Dan said.

The casualties had created unpleasant duties for them to perform. Dan, Flagg, and the other men spent the morning burying the dead. Simon's resting place overlooked the southern landscape near where Dan had stood the first day he arrived. He thought it was a good choice. They gathered around and listened as Ash read Scripture, and after the last ''Amen'' they returned to their own lives, leaving Simon to the land.

Dan noticed that Allander was keeping to himself. All the hot air was gone from the man, and he wore a morose expression. Dan figured this had been his first battle, his first brush with death.

On the walk back from the grave site, he noticed that Tony's shoulders had slumped, and that she was putting one foot in front of the other as if it were a great chore to do so. He wished that he could do something to cheer her up, for this was the second time in the days since he'd known her that she had to suffer grief. But the fact was there wasn't a thing he could do. Again, grief had to be left to time.

At daybreak he left the bunkhouse and went to the corral. There he picked out a new mount, for while the dun had come back, it needed a rest. While he was tightening the cinch he got some unexpected company. It was Kearney.

"Looks like you're getting ready to go somewhere."

"Thought I'd take a ride today."

"Well, you picked a good horse. That sabino likes to run. Give him his head and he can outrun anything we got."

That was good to know. Its speed and stamina might save him.

"I'm going to need another one too."

Kearney pointed to an Appaloosa.

"That one over there. He'll do."

Dan approached and patted the Appaloosa's neck. He was nuzzled as a reward. Kearney brought him an old saddle and bridle from the barn, and Dan got the second horse ready to ride.

"Are you taking somebody with you, or are you going to bring somebody back here?" asked the Irishman.

"If I'm real lucky, neither one. I'm going to try to haul one bad hombre down to Fort Verde."

Kearney slapped his thigh and chortled.

"Well, I'll be . . . It's not that I don't admire your spunk, but just how do you aim to get that hombre to go with you? In fact, how do you invite him?"

"I haven't exactly got that worked out yet. What I plan to do is to be at the right place at the right time and watch for an opportunity."

"Well, if I can't convince you otherwise," Kearney said as he held out his hand, "then I wish you luck."

"Thanks," said Dan, grasping it. "I've got a feeling I'm going to need lots of it."

Dan slipped into the house before he left and got

Ash to fill a bag with edibles. With that, and a couple of canteens of water, he rode away on the sabino, leading the spare. He took a circuitous route toward Keaton's stronghold. He figured it was his best bet for not being spotted or ambushed.

He expected that Emma knew her former employer pretty well, and if Keaton was mad before, he'd be doubly so, now. Not only had he failed to burn the Quigleys out, he was short by three men. There was no telling what revenge his anger would drive him to seek. It was this threat that had prompted Dan's decision to go after him.

The morning sky was overcast, something that he was unaccustomed to seeing since he'd arrived in Arizona Territory. The low gray shroud looked to be just above the tree line. He felt a chill in the air that seemed to be growing colder by the hour. As he pulled up the collar of his coat for greater warmth, he asked himself how many days had passed since he'd been sweating his way across the desert. The answer was, not many. But in a way, they seemed to him like a whole lifetime.

The fall days had grown shorter, and since the day was a dark one to begin with, there wasn't a lot of light left when he looked out on the cluster of buildings in the distance that made up the Keaton stronghold. This was good. He was less likely to be seen, and it meant he would have a shorter wait before he moved in.

He dismounted, and when his legs grew tired, he sank into a squatting position. With the help of his field glasses he was able to watch the comings and goings. The gang had found their way home, and he counted a total of seven. Certainly, there could be others around that he hadn't spotted. None appeared to be worried about an attack. He didn't expect that Keaton or Draper, either one, would imagine that a crippled enemy could pose an immediate threat. This was to his advantage as, again, he was about to do the unexpected.

Only one bored looking guard huddled in his coat near the door of the main house. The others had gone inside the bunkhouse. The cold discouraged them from lingering outside. Without the moon, or even a few stars peeking through the cloud cover, the darkness was almost complete.

At the house, someone had lighted a coal oil lamp. It was time for him to move.

He rode the sabino from his hiding place, leading the Appaloosa. Silently, carefully he traversed the open space that lay between himself and Noah Keaton. When he'd approached as close as he dared on horseback, he left the sabino and the Appaloosa, and went the rest of the way on foot. When he reached the side of the house, he hugged the wall and held his breath.

Relieved that there was no shout of alarm or sound of running boots, he slipped his knife from beneath his belt. There was no other sound except the boisterous voices coming from the bunkhouse.

With every nerve taut, he stepped to the corner of the house. The solitary guard had his back to Dan. With a giant step and a single motion of his arm, the knife was at the guard's neck. The man froze, without so much as a gurgle escaping from his throat. In a kind of lockstep, Dan backed him away from the house into deeper darkness. When they got all the way to the horses, he stopped.

"If you want to live to see another day, *amigo*, you'll keep quiet and lie down on the ground," he whispered.

He moved the knife away from the outlaw's throat, but was careful to let him feel the point in its new position at his back. The outlaw did as he was told. Dan tied him up with piggin' strings. Then he took the man's bandanna and gagged him.

"Just stay there and don't make any trouble, and you might live through this," he advised the outlaw softly.

Again, Dan slipped back to the house. One down and one to go, he counted to himself. He hoped that his luck would hold out for a little while longer. He was about to go around the corner, when he heard a door squeak open. Across the clearing, a man came out of the barn. He paused and lighted a cigarette that he must have just made before stepping outside. The match was extinguished, and the red tip glowed in the darkness. Dan kept his eyes averted from the light. While the man at the barn stood enjoying his smoke, sheltered from the wind by the door, Dan tried to make himself invisible against the house. Each minute seemed like an eternity, until the smoker finally tossed the remains of his cigarette away. Having satisfied his craving, he crossed the distance to the bunkhouse and went inside.

Dan stepped around the corner and tapped lightly on the door.

"What do you want?" Keaton yelled from inside.

He got no answer.

Dan stood aside from the door, knife in hand, waiting. He heard the squeak of a leather chair as a large bulk was lifted from it. Heavy footsteps trudged across the floor. Suddenly, the door was jerked open.

"Dorsey, I told you that I don't . . ."

Keaton found that he was addressing empty space. He stepped outside to find Dorsey. Dan brought the knife to the outlaw's throat. He could feel Keaton's scarcely restrained rage. It was mixed with fear.

"This way," Dan whispered in his ear, "and quietly if you want to live."

He retraced the steps he'd taken with the guard, and soon Keaton was tied and gagged, as well. The noise from the bunkhouse was becoming more raucous. The ones inside were intent on their entertainment, and they'd never hear two horses leaving. He hoisted Keaton onto the back of the Appaloosa like he was a big sack of grain. It wasn't an easy task, especially since he wasn't of a mind to cooperate. It took the point of Dan's knife to change Keaton's attitude.

"I'm leaving now," he told the guard, who hadn't moved a muscle as far as he could tell. "You'd better make sure that I'm far, far away before you let out so much as a whimper. Otherwise, I'll come back and kill you."

Dan threw his leg over the sabino and led the Appaloosa away. He headed due south, looking back from time to time. When he could no longer see the light from the kerosene lamp in the house, he allowed himself to think that he just might have gotten away with the outlaw's abduction.

He picked his way carefully in the darkness. From time to time he heard noises coming from behind Keaton's gag. It appeared that the outlaw didn't like his position and intended that Dan should know it.

"Quit your complaining," he said. "You could do a lot worse. I could haul you off that horse and make you walk the rest of the way."

Keaton started thrashing around.

"I guess you want me to prove it to you," he threatened.

The thrashing stopped.

The snow started. The storm had held off longer than he'd had any right to expect, so he wasn't complaining. Another time, he'd appreciate its beauty. Tonight, it was a threat. It was easy to get lost inside the falling white curtain and ride in circles. He needed to find shelter for himself and the horses, and his prisoner too, for he intended to turn Keaton over alive and in as good a shape as possible to the authorities at Fort Verde. As it turned out, it was the sabino that found shelter for them. The big horse slid down the steep side of a hollow. At the bottom there was relief from the north wind. Now Dan had a fighting chance against the elements for the night. It seemed that Nature herself had become his enemy.

Chapter Ten

Tony heard Kearney come inside the barn. She watched through half-closed lids as he took down an old saddle and went back outside with it. Kicking her covers aside, she scurried to the door and peeked out. Dan was getting two horses ready to ride. Who was going with him, she wondered. Kearney? And where were they going?

To her surprise, Kearney stayed behind. After stopping off at the house for a few minutes, Dan rode out alone, leading the Appaloosa.

She had to know what was going on. Before Kearney could get away, she cornered him at the corral.

"Where was Dan headed to?" she demanded.

Kearney looked like he badly wanted to be somewhere else, anywhere else.

"If you have to know, he's got this notion that he's going over to the Circle K and capture Keaton. Then he's taking him to Fort Verde to stand trial."

"Alone? He's insane."

"Maybe."

"Why didn't you stop him?"

Kearney shrugged.

"He's as smart as they come, and he just might get the job done."

"I think he will," said Emma, who'd come up behind her and was wearing one of her grandfather's shirts. "None of that outfit will be expecting him, and he has the advantage of surprise."

All of the anger that Tony had felt for the woman had vanished. Too much had happened. Now she felt only pity for what Emma had been through.

"I hope you're right," she said.

"Of course I'm right. Now, why don't you come to the house, and I'll fix you some breakfast."

Tony realized that she was hungry, and the idea appealed to her.

Inside the house, Emma scrambled eggs with bits of bacon. Ash had left, and the place was theirs, for a time at least. When the food was ready, Emma put the plates, along with cups of hot coffee on the table. The women sat across from each other.

"Do you believe in fate?" the older woman asked.

The question took Tony by surprise. She believed more in personal choice, in happenstance, and perhaps in luck, but she hedged.

"Maybe."

Emma peered into her cup as if trying to find the words that she needed somewhere in the dark liquid.

"After Lester died," she said at last, "I thought I could make out of my life what I wanted. What I wanted most was security, and a man to provide that security. I believed that Noah Keaton was going to be that man. But no matter how hard I tried, I got nothing but rejection and abuse. The reason that it didn't work out was fate. I'd simply been wasting my time.''

Tony figured the reason it hadn't worked out was because Emma had made a misguided choice, but she didn't say so.

''Some people believe in fate, I guess,'' she said instead.

Emma must have sensed her skepticism, for she tried again.

''A good example of its power is your grandfather's determination to send you back east. It wasn't meant to be, and so it didn't happen.''

Emma couldn't have picked a better argument to convince Tony. Her escape from being dumped into Eastern society had been a close one. Still, she credited that escape to luck.

''What I'm getting at,'' Emma went on, ''is that I believe it's Dan's fate to capture Keaton and bring him to justice. I don't think anything can stop him.''

''Well, he did cross our path just when we needed him the most,'' Tony conceded.

Emma accepted the point graciously.

''Now, all you have to do is surrender to fate and stop worrying.''

That might be all right for Emma, but giving up wasn't any part of Tony's nature. Emma was welcome to her philosophy about surrendering to some invisible force, but Tony intended to stick with reality.

''Speaking of fate,'' she said, ''what about you and Grandpa?''

"What do you mean?" asked Emma, who appeared flustered by the question.

"He likes you."

Emma blushed, and Tony enjoyed her discomfiture.

"There's nothing between us," she said. "Asher is a gentleman. He's always treated me with respect and kindness. That's all there is to it."

Tony leaned back, toying with the pottery cup that she held.

"I wouldn't be too sure. Grandpa isn't rich, but maybe he will be someday. You could do a whole lot worse than to marry him."

She could tell that the idea appealed to Emma.

"I would think you'd be against our marriage."

"Actually, I think Grandpa needs a wife. You'd be good for him."

Emma smiled, and it was beautiful. It made Tony feel pretty good about herself and her change of attitude.

"I guess I'll just have to wait for Asher to decide that for himself," Emma said. "It wouldn't do for me to propose to him, now would it?"

As far as Tony was concerned, it didn't make any difference who proposed as long as a couple got together.

After they'd finished and Tony had offered to help clean up, Emma shooed her outside.

"I know you've got other things that need doin'," she'd said.

That was true enough.

The morning slipped away, and in the afternoon

when she was stacking the wood, she noticed that the temperature was dropping.

"Better get your heavy coat on, missy," Ash said when he passed by on his way to the house. "There's going to be snow falling before long."

She figured he was right, for the clouds looked almost low enough to touch, and there was that expectancy in the air that forewarned of an impending storm. She worried about Dan, who was sure to be caught out in it.

She'd let herself hope that he would come to his senses and return to the ranch, but that hadn't happened. He was actually going through with his scheme. If the weather weren't so threatening, she'd ask Aaron, and maybe Flagg, to go after him. She'd even considered going herself. But it would be too late now. Dan was probably at the Circle K already, and whatever was going to happen was happening.

Before her, the blade of an ax was buried in a stump. She grabbed hold of the handle and pulled it loose, pretending that she was King Arthur pulling the sword from the stone. The sense of empowerment that she'd hoped for didn't come.

She looked up to see Aaron riding into the clearing.

"I thought you went with Jacob to take Eloy's place," she said accusingly as he rode up to where she was standing, ax in hand.

"It's always nice to feel welcome," he teased.

She lifted the ax over her head and slammed it back into the stump.

"I helped take some supplies, but Eloy wanted to

stay, and I wanted to come back,'' Aaron said as he swung down from the horse.

"I met Kearney on the way in, and he said that Dan had gone off to the enemy camp to drag Keaton down to Fort Verde.''

"More or less, I guess that's what happened.''

"Thought maybe I'd take a little ride in that direction myself.''

She felt hope stirring inside her.

"Oh, would you?''

"As soon as I get something hot to eat, and providing I don't get lost in that storm that's comin' in.''

"I don't suppose you'd take me with you?'' she asked tentatively.

"You suppose right,'' Aaron said. "I don't want your grandpa parting my hair with his rifle for dragging you off to someplace dangerous.''

"Then be careful, and do the best you can. He might need help.''

Aaron nodded and then went in the direction of food.

It was right at dark when she watched him ride out. Soon afterward, large flakes of snow began falling. She wondered if she'd regret urging Aaron to go on what her grandfather had called a "fool's mission.'' Maybe, but she hadn't known what else to do. She hated feeling helpless, hated it more than poison. If she never accomplished anything else in her entire life, she was going to overcome helplessness.

Chapter Eleven

It would have been difficult enough working in the darkness, but working in the middle of a snowstorm was even worse. Dan had no choice. He gathered needle-thick branches and wove them into a shelter. His worn gloves failed to warm his hands, and he forced sluggish fingers to work quickly. When the make-do shelter was finished, he dragged Keaton's bulk inside. Then he built a fire near the opening. The horses moved in close to take advantage of the warmth. With luck, he figured they'd make it through until daylight.

Keaton thrashed around on the ground, uttering muffled curses under his gag.

"If you'll shut up, I'll take it off," Dan said.

His promise met with a welcome silence, so Dan squatted down and removed the bandanna, hoping the silence would last.

He put some coffee on the fire to boil. When it was finished, he drank a cup of the hot, reviving liquid, letting it fill his whole being with warmth. Then he reached over and poured the cup full again.

"Behave yourself, and you can have this," he told Keaton. "I'll untie you, but just remember, all the time I'll have you covered."

The outlaw snarled, but otherwise held his tongue. They were seated on opposite sides of the shelter, which meant there was about a foot of ground separating them. When he'd drained the cup, and Dan was tying his wrists again, he started in with threats.

"I guess you know that you're a dead man."

"We've all got to die sometime," Dan replied.

"You're not going to have to wait very long. Ben Draper will see to that."

"Yeah?"

"He says that he remembers you well, and he's been planning on looking you up for old times' sake."

"I guess maybe he didn't tell you. He's already found me."

Keaton looked surprised.

"What are you talking about?"

"He ambushed me the other day when I was on my way to the Barton place. It made me plumb mad, and I ran him off. The last I saw of him was the backside of his horse hightailing it toward your ranch."

This was obviously news to Keaton, and it was news he didn't like to hear.

"You're lying," he accused. "Draper never said anything about it."

Dan tossed some twigs on the fire to keep it going.

"Did you expect that he would? A man's not likely to go around bragging about his failures, now is he."

"Why, that yellow-bellied coward . . . ," he started.

"Well," Dan said, "I've always heard that 'like' attracts 'like'."

That started a string of expletives, and Dan reached over and stuffed the gag back into his mouth.

The rest of the night passed slowly and uncomfortably. He dared not let himself doze off until he heard Keaton's regular breathing. Figuring it was safe to do so, he pulled the gag off again, and was rewarded with some first-rate snoring. After that, Dan slept lightly and fitfully. From time to time he fed the fire to keep it going. When it felt like he'd been huddled in the shelter at least a week, he crawled outside to have a look around. He saw the reason why it had grown colder. The cloud cover was gone and he was able to see the last of the stars. Without those clouds, it was going to be a bright day—blinding bright.

Inside the pile of branches, Keaton was stirring to wakefulness.

Dan put on more coffee to boil, and they breakfasted on that and cold biscuits.

The storm of the night before had wiped out any trail they might have left. If Keaton's men had a mind to follow, they'd have to do it "by guess and by golly," at least until they happened onto the wash and the remains of the shelter. From then on it'd be easy to follow the tracks in the snow. He had to get his prisoner as far away as he could, as soon as possible. After some prodding, Keaton was sitting upright in the saddle of the Appaloosa. Dan mounted

the sabino, and they headed in the direction of Fort
Verde. Just ahead lay Captain Timberlake's land.
Dan would have to cross it, but with a little luck the
captain would never know, and therefore remain
uninvolved.

The wound in Dan's side was bothering him again
after the long hours in the saddle and the cold, miserable night in the shelter. He was aware that his
wound could have been worse, though, or fatal. And
while life wasn't always easy, and sometimes it was
downright unpleasant, he knew that he very much
wanted to live.

The sparkling blanket of snow over which they
traveled was like a giant mirror reflecting the rays
of the sun. It wasn't long before Keaton was
complaining.

"This blasted glare is blinding me," he said.

"Shut your eyes," Dan said. This was advice that
he took himself from time to time to relieve his own
suffering.

Anyone who followed would be faced with the
same handicap. Right now, his ears were better
guardians. Every so often, he would make Keaton
stop and be quiet. Then he would listen for sounds
of pursuit. Always, he was met with silence.

"When my men catch up with you," Keaton said
after one such pause, "they're going to hang you."

"Silence!" Dan said.

The outlaw spat into the snow, showing his contempt as they started on.

During the ride across Timberlake land, Dan
didn't spot a soul. This was a relief to him, for he

couldn't count on the captain not to cause trouble in the name of neutrality.

About the time the sun reached its zenith, he felt a warm wind blowing from the south. Soon there were signs of melting snow. In places that got a lot of exposure, the ground was mushy under the horses' hooves. Dan was concerned, for if the snow-melt froze again in the nighttime temperatures it would form ice, and a bit of hidden ice could cause a horse to slip and break a leg.

To his advantage, he figured he was out of Timberlake's domain by now, and so far Draper hadn't picked up his trail.

"You planning on eating any time soon?" Keaton asked. "Or are you going to try to starve me to death?"

"You'd have to miss a lot more meals than one before you starve," Dan shot back.

Keaton's girth was evidently a sore spot.

"You know, Newland, killing you is going to give me a lot of pleasure some day. I regret that I paid Draper all that gold to do it for me. Maybe I'll just have to take it back."

"Have fun tryin' on both counts," Dan said. "But killing me won't be easy, and I doubt that Draper is going to hand over any gold just because you say, 'pretty please.' "

Dan let out more lead rope then, and rode as far ahead of the Appaloosa as its length would allow.

He was hungry himself, though, and when he found a spot that would give him some protection, he stopped. There he shared jerky and biscuits with the outlaw.

He had no doubt that the guard he'd left behind had either worked himself loose, or had gotten the attention of somebody else to cut him free. Probably in record time, since he was highly motivated. Only the storm had prevented an immediate chase. The storm had also covered his trail. He wondered how long Draper, who was surely the self-appointed leader now, would wander around before he stumbled onto the remains of his camp in the hollow.

Draper would be smart enough to know that he wouldn't drag Keaton back to the Lazy Q, thereby bringing more trouble to the Quigleys' doorstep. But he might also be smart enough to think of Fort Verde and a trial. With that in mind, his old enemy would come closer to searching in the right place for his tracks.

This part of the country was unfamiliar to Dan. He knew the general direction in which Fort Verde was located, and about how far it was, but that was all. Indians were always a danger too, and with Keaton watching for any means of escape, Dan had his work cut out.

Not long before he lost the light, Dan happened onto a place that would do for a camp. It was a windblown indentation in a wall of brownish red stone that was almost a cave. It would protect him and the horses from the elements, and hide them from his enemies, both outlaws and Apaches.

He decided to risk a fire, for it would be impossible to see it from the north, and it was unlikely to be seen from the south. Again, they ate the scanty provisions from his saddlebags. Again Keaton complained. But the day had taken its toll, and the outlaw, after having filled his belly, soon slept.

Dan sat with his back against the cold stone, his rifle at his knee. Unlike the night before, this night was clear, and diamonds sparkled in a heaven of black velvet. He thought of Tony and wondered what she was doing. Had she made her peace with Emma, or was she still holed up in the barn? Tony was a difficult person to know, but he had to admit that she was well worth the effort it took.

He finally succumbed to exhaustion and dozed, always lightly, always for just a short time. It was during one of these flirtations with sleep that he was alerted by a noise. His head jerked up, and he looked over at Keaton, who appeared to be sleeping soundly. He tightened his grip on the rifle and got to his feet. Silently he moved to the edge of the indented wall to scan the dark landscape. Everything within his hearing and range of vision was still. The noise could have been made by a nocturnal creature hunting for his dinner, he decided, or maybe the wind had knocked some snow from a limb. Still, he couldn't afford to ignore it. While remaining in the deeper darkness against the cave wall, he picked up a rock and tossed it outside the amphitheater like opening. Response was immediate. A bullet plowed through the dirt where the stone had landed. The report roused his prisoner, who rolled back as far away from the mouth of their shelter as possible.

"Are you in there, Keaton?" came Draper's shout.

Before Dan could stop him, Keaton called out that he was.

"Be careful where you're shooting," he warned the gunman.

Dan wondered how many were with him. How many would follow Draper's orders and go riding off on an unmarked blanket of white with no trail to follow, at least not until it was discovered miles away from their starting point?

"Give it up, Newland. You don't have a chance."

Dan wasn't about to give up to Draper, who wanted him dead, and was being paid in gold to do the job. Better to be shot with a gun in his hand. One thing was for sure, he intended to make the gunman work for his gold.

At the moment, though, they appeared to be locked in a standoff. Dan peered into the darkness, and for an instant he thought he saw Draper's outline where a mesquite moved without the benefit of the wind. He aimed the rifle, but before he could fire it, his head exploded in a burst of lights. The light display was followed by intolerable pain. Then everything went dark.

Chapter Twelve

Noah had been holding his breath, but now he was panting from his exertions. At his feet lay the inert body of his captor. Swinging that rock to the back of Newland's head had given him considerable satisfaction. It was little enough repayment for his own torn and bloody wrists from working off the bindings. For his kidnapping and humiliation there would be a greater payment later.

"Hold your fire!" he shouted to Draper. "Newland won't trouble you. He's out cold."

He listened as Draper moved cautiously through the darkness. The sounds were slight.

"It's about time you showed up," Noah complained as soon as Draper's form appeared. "What took you so long, and where's the rest of the outfit?"

Ignoring him, Draper turned instead to the unconscious man and disarmed him. Then he faced Noah in the moonlight.

"Do you think those saddle bums you hired were going to go chasin' after you in a blizzard? I didn't leave, myself, until the storm quit. When I did start out, I figured I'd do a whole lot better on my own. I could move quieter that way, and if any shootin' needed to be done, I could do it from ambush and get out pronto.''

Noah conceded to Draper's judgment. The rest of his outfit amounted to nothing more than strong backs and trigger fingers, anyway. Draper was the only smart one in the bunch. He reminded himself that Draper's intelligence was something he'd better not ever forget.

''I can earn my money right now,'' said the gunman. ''Want me to put a bullet into him?''

''Not now. Not after what he's done to me. I intend to make him real sorry about living before he dies.''

There was enough moonlight that he could see the Texan shrug.

''Have it your way,'' Draper said. ''But remember that whatever happens, you owe me the other half of the gold we agreed on. I've kept my part of the deal.''

Noah still needed Draper. He dared not let him get suspicious.

''That's so,'' he said in as soothing a voice as he could manage, ''and when we get back to the ranch, I'll give it to you.''

The tension in Draper's body relaxed. The assurance appeared to satisfy him, but with the gunman, he could never be sure.

Noah nudged Newland's body with the toe of his boot.

''Tie him up,'' he ordered. ''Come daylight, we'll throw him across the saddle. That way he can enjoy the same kind of ride that I had to endure in that miserable snowstorm.''

''Unless he improves some, it don't look to me like he's going to care one way or the other how he rides.''

Noah felt a sense of victory coursing through him.

''Oh, he will. Before I'm through with him, he's going to care a whole lot.'' He was referring to more than the trip.

Draper laughed quietly. ''I wouldn't spread it around to the neighbors, but I think you got a mean streak in you.''

Noah ignored him.

''Newland built a fire,'' Draper observed.

''Yeah. But I could tell he was afraid that you and the others might spot it. He was just plain scared.''

''It turned out he had a right to be. But there's Apaches around too. I heard talk.''

Any mention of Apache made Noah nervous. He'd seen what they did to their victims.

''I've always heard they wouldn't attack at night,'' he said, trying to keep his voice steady.

''It ain't going to be night forever.''

That single, ominous statement robbed him of his sense of satisfaction and rekindled fear.

''It'll be dawn before long. We'd better get out of here at first light.''

''Between now and then,'' Draper said, ''I intend to get some rest. By the way, I sleep real light, so don't try anything foolish.''

Noah was glad it was dark, for the thought had slid across the surface of his mind, and Draper would surely have read his expression.

For something distracting to do, and not wanting his enemy to die prematurely, he picked up a blanket and threw it over Newland's body.

While Draper settled himself down near the entrance, Noah chose the back where he could watch both Newland and the gunman. So far, the Lazy Q foreman had showed no signs of consciousness. For the rest of the night, Noah kept watch. All the while, he yearned for the taste of one of his imported cigars.

At dawn, the two of them hoisted about 170 pounds of dead weight across the white-bellied horse. Newland was still alive, though, and Noah thought he heard a low moan while they were moving him. Just before they rode out, Draper took a spyglass and made a sweep of the terrain.

"See anything?" Noah asked anxiously.

"No."

That simple word was a big relief.

They went back the same way they'd come. Draper had the sabino on a lead rope. The sky was unclouded, the air was growing warmer, and Noah figured that before nightfall the snow cover would disappear.

He glanced back at the horse that Draper was leading. From time to time, he thought he detected signs that Newland was working his way to consciousness. Good.

It was a few hours after they'd left the camp when Draper pulled up and signaled for silence. While Noah stayed with the prisoner, Draper dismounted and crawled to the top of a gentle hill. Noah could feel the sweat forming on his brow and under his collar. He loosed the thong on the holster that he'd taken from Newland.

Draper lay near the crest of the hill, watching. That could mean only one thing. A raiding party had picked up their trail. Or maybe they were on the trail of bigger game. It was a slim hope and the closest that Noah had come to a prayer since the day he'd fled the city

Chapter Thirteen

A swirling curtain of fog blinded Dan. He struggled, trying to find his way through it. His head hurt, and intense cold penetrated his flesh. He was shivering, but he kept on searching for a recognizable landmark. He wondered how long he could endure being lost in this strange place. He sensed that the answer was not long at all. Then the fog was replaced by darkness.

He had no idea of how much time had passed when the darkness lifted and he opened his eyes. He became aware of the rhythmic gait of a horse beneath his body. His head ached, and the ache was aggravated by the position of his head. Both his vision and his mind started to clear. Keaton must have gotten loose somehow and hit him from behind. So the shoe was on the other foot now, and he was the prisoner of two men who wanted him dead. He kept still and feigned unconsciousness, for this was his only advantage.

Suddenly the horse stopped, flinging Dan against the ropes that tied him in place. Through tiny slits, he tried to see what was going on. Keaton was on the Appaloosa, and he was holding the reins of Draper's mount and the lead rope to the sabino. Keaton's attention was focused in the distance, and Dan risked moving his head a couple of inches so he could see what the outlaw was looking at.

Draper was climbing a low hill on foot, trying to make himself as much a part of the landscape as possible. When he could see over the crest, he lay there watching. A minute or two passed before he slid back down and ran for his horse.

"They're out there," he said in a low voice.

"Do they know we're here?"

"Possibly. I ain't taking any chances. Let's get our backsides out of here."

Keaton started to hand the lead rope to Draper, and looked startled when the gunman slapped it out of his hand.

"Leave him. We won't have a chance dragging him along with us."

"No, I won't leave him," Keaton said. "He's mine."

It was the quietest argument that Dan had heard in a long time.

"What do you think you can do to him that the Apaches won't?" Draper asked.

Keaton remembered the Apache wrath and he felt further motivated to get his own hide out of there. He turned away from the sabino to find that Draper was already leading his own mount in the opposite direction with as much haste and as much silence as possible. Keaton followed.

Dan was left tied like a bag of barley, unarmed,

on the back of a worn-out horse. Just beyond that hill, somewhere, there was a band of hostile Indians who would like to add another scalp to their collection. He fought back the panic that rose like bile. Words that his father had told him years ago came to mind.

"You can tell the worth of a man, son, by the way he behaves when everything's going against him."

Well, things couldn't be going against him worse than they were at the moment. He pulled against the ropes that held him in an act of desperation and found that they were loosely tied. They'd been meant simply as a measure to keep him from falling off, and the weight of his body being thrown against them during the journey had loosened them even more. He managed to pull them off and to slide from the back of the sabino. His hands and feet were still tied, and he needed a hiding place. He didn't have many choices.

He half-scooted, half-rolled until he was hidden in a patch of scrub. Thankfully the snow was gone and the grass had dried in the sunshine. This wouldn't save him from a good tracker, but at least the trail he'd left wasn't screaming his whereabouts, as it would have done in mud or snow. Riderless, the sabino had wandered off. Maybe the raiding party would go after Keaton and Draper and overlook him. It was a measure of hope. Or maybe the Apache had something else in mind that brought them up here.

He heard them then. That meant they didn't suspect that anyone was here. They were close, though—just beyond the rise that Draper had climbed. He held his breath and listened to the blood pound inside his throbbing head. Then he realized that they weren't coming his way at all. He let his breath out slowly, feeling a sense of relief. They were heading toward the Timberlake ranch. He tried to recall how many men the captain had to defend the place, for it looked like the man so intent on minding his own business was going to have to make a stand after all.

When he could no longer hear the sounds of the raiding party, Dan pushed himself to a sitting position and groped for the knife that he'd hidden in his boot. Maybe the outlaws had failed to search there in their flush of victory. His fingers touched the handle. Luck was with him, still.

When he was free, he rubbed the circulation back into his limbs and took stock of his situation. He was somewhere to the southwest of the Timberlake place. He had no weapons, save the knife, and no food or water. Worst of all, he had no horse. His prisoner had gotten away from him, and all of his time and effort had been wasted. For once, he was glad that his father wasn't around to see what kind of mess he was in. He doubted that August Newland would be impressed.

There was nothing he could do to warn Timberlake in time. He knew that his reprieve would be short if Draper and Keaton got up the nerve to come back to find out what had happened to him. He took a deep breath to clear his head and started walking.

He thought of young Stringbean, of Barnabas, and Lucas. He wondered how these Timberlake hands would fare in the attack. He wished that he could warn them. He wondered if the captain was well prepared.

Not wanting to run into the Apache on their return, he kept far to the west, but not so far that his other enemies would come upon him if they decided to backtrack. He was hungry, and he wanted a drink—of anything. It was afternoon when Aaron found him.

"You look like you've been havin' yourself a good time, Dan," Aaron said in greeting. He held the lead rope with the sabino attached to it.

"Got a canteen?" Dan asked ignoring the banter. After food and water, he felt more like talking.

"What brings you out this way?" he asked when he was astride a horse again.

"I just can't ignore the pleas of a lady in distress."

Tony. She'd sent Aaron after him.

"Does Ash know?"

"I expect he does by now."

By mutual unspoken consent, they headed in the direction of the TL ranch.

"You were out in the storm," Dan said.

"Yep. It was right pretty. But it does tend to cover up tracks."

"How did you find me?"

"Tony said that you planned to take Keaton to Fort Verde and turn him over to the authorities. I figured you could handle the part about fetching him away from his ranch, but I thought you might like to have some company on the way south. It wasn't hard to determine the shortest route from Keaton's place to the fort. It was along that line that I started lookin'.''

''Anything to please a lady in distress.''

Aaron looked embarrassed.

''Actually, I figured it was a good way to get out of work and take a nice ride through the countryside.''

Dan managed a chuckle, which made his head hurt. Then he began to dread what they might find at the captain's place. What they found exceeded his worst fears. The structures, including the main house, had been burned to the ground, and they were still smoking. Bodies littered the place. The stock had been taken by the attackers, and the only signs of life were some vultures.

They all had died fighting, even old Lucas and young Stringbean.

''We've got to get 'em underground,'' said Aaron, who looked sick.

Dan agreed. They dug a trench for a communal grave to save the remains from the vultures. He figured he'd dug enough graves in the last couple of weeks to last him a lifetime.

The one bright spot in the whole tragedy was the evidence that the captain had found his courage and had gone down fighting.

''What now?'' Aaron asked when they were well away from the sight and smell of the carnage.

Dan had asked himself the same question. They had no choice but to leave the raiders to General Crook and the Army. It would only be a matter of time before they were brought to justice. Right now, he had other enemies to deal with.

"We can't let Keaton get away," he said. "So far, he's had everything going for him, and he's drunk with power."

"Then let's get him."

Dan stopped abruptly.

"Aaron, I want you to ride on to the ranch by yourself. Tell Ash that I want Flagg, Allander, and Kearney to go with you to the Circle K. I'm on my way now, and I'll keep out of sight and wait for you."

"How many men do you think Keaton has left?"

"When I was watching the place," Dan said, "I counted seven. Keaton would make eight. There might be more, but they weren't around the other night."

"Those odds aren't too bad—five to eight."

Dan noticed that Aaron's spirits were perking up now that he had a job to do. He disagreed with Aaron's assessment of the odds, but the four men he'd have on his side were all dependable and highly motivated. That had to count for something.

"What do you intend to do at the enemy camp while I'm gathering the troops?" Aaron asked.

"Probably just lie low and keep an eye on what's going on."

"Don't let 'em catch you," Aaron said, and with that warning and a quick salute, he was gone.

Dan turned north. What supplies he had left were still in his saddlebags. Although Keaton had taken his pistol, he'd left his rifle in its scabbard on the sabino for the sake of convenience. Neither Keaton nor Draper had expected Dan would ever be using it again. Without the .45 Dan felt ill prepared for trouble. But the rifle would do.

Chapter Fourteen

Dan spent the night in his bedroll, letting his body rest and his head recover from the blow. By late afternoon on the following day, he was in woods that paralleled the Circle K. He chose a place where he could observe the ranch without being seen. He fished the field glasses from his pack and settled down to watch. However, the tableau he viewed puzzled him. Draper was standing in plain sight giving orders to the other hands, but Keaton was absent. When the others had scattered to do his bidding, instead of going to the bunkhouse, Draper went straight to the main house that Keaton had occupied. He walked right in without knocking, just as if he owned the place. Shortly after sunset, a lamp was lighted inside. Then Draper appeared in the doorway. He lounged against the frame as he smoked a cigar. The only possible explanation for Draper's proprietary behavior, coupled with Keaton's absence, was that Keaton was dead.

Dan remembered how he'd bragged about paying Draper in gold. Maybe Draper decided that he

162

wanted all of Keaton's gold rather than just a payment. It looked like he'd taken over the ranch, as well.

Dan figured that after they'd spotted the Apache and left him, Draper would have had his best opportunity for the kill. Sight of the raiding party had scared Keaton out of his wits, and he'd started depending on Draper, lowering his guard. Killing him would have been easy, especially for someone with Draper's turn of mind. Considering what probably happened, it seemed that Keaton had received a kind of justice after all. One thing was for sure, Dan couldn't work up any pity for the man who'd left him behind for the Apache.

It was only Draper that he had to deal with now, the same as when he'd left Fort Yuma. The difference was that Draper had six of Keaton's men to back him up. Well, Dan's hand had improved as well. That is, as soon as Aaron arrived with the others.

He continued to keep watch as the outlaw finished his smoke and went back inside, closing the door against the cold. Dan wondered if Keaton had hidden his gold somewhere in the house. If not, it was undoubtedly close by. Since Draper wasn't tearing the place apart looking for it, he'd most likely discovered its whereabouts.

Dan put the glasses away, for darkness rendered them useless. Then he leaned against a tree trunk and continued the vigil without them. The men made their way to the bunkhouse after they'd eaten, and he heard the sounds of laughter and voices. But in time, the noise stopped, and the light went out. It was much later when the lamp was snuffed in the main house.

The moon had risen, and it cast enough light for him to see the door open. Draper emerged carrying two heavy-looking saddlebags. The gunman went straight to the barn, and when he came out he was leading a horse.

Dan got up and struggled to walk on feet that had gone to sleep. He put his hand on the reins of the sabino, for it looked like he was about to take a moonlight ride. He watched as Draper led his horse well past the bunkhouse before he mounted and headed north. Quietly Dan rode along the edge of the woods, keeping enough distance between himself and Draper so that the gunman wouldn't suspect he was being followed.

Aaron and the others would fail to find him waiting at the agreed-on spot, but he couldn't worry about that. From the weight of the saddlebags that Draper was carrying, Dan suspected they were filled with gold, and that the outlaw was on his way to stash it.

Draper was heading in the general direction of the valley where Dan had been wounded, but he doubted if Draper intended to go that far. He'd need to stay close to the ranch, for his prolonged absence might well emboldened the others to take it over.

Dan kept to the deeper shadows as moonlight spilled like liquid silver across the high meadows. The wind came up, scattering in its wake the scent of moisture and pine needles. Clouds formed causing starless patches in the sky.

When the outlaw had traveled farther than expected, Dan began to wonder if Draper intended to go back at all. Maybe the cache of gold had been enough for him, and he was making his getaway. He dismissed the idea, for it was unlikely that Draper would turn his back on everything Keaton had amassed. For one thing, it was there simply for the taking. For another, Draper was almost as greedy and power-hungry as his predecessor.

Up ahead his quarry turned off to the right, placing a stand of trees between himself and Dan. At that moment, the cloud that was moving across the moon completely obscured it, leaving only a few stars to light the land. He nudged the sabino forward and took a shortcut through the trees. Beneath the branches, it was dark as a pit at midnight. When he emerged on the other side, there was no sign of Draper. The cloud moved on, giving Earth back her nightlight, but it was too late. The outlaw had disappeared. Dan paused and was listening for sounds that would give Draper away, when a muffled footfall warned him. Dan reached for the rifle.

"Don't try it!" ordered Draper's voice in the darkness. Dan froze, his hand inches away from the weapon.

Draper emerged from the shadows where he'd waited. When he saw that Dan was the one who'd been following him, he acted like he couldn't believe what he was seeing.

"Well, well, Newland, you surprise me. I've got to admit that you're uncommonly good at surviving. I can see that I'm going to have to be real careful and take some special pains with you."

"Shooting a man face-to-face just doesn't appeal to you anymore does it, Draper?" he prodded.

"Nope. Too much risk and no profit at all."

"How did your boss get it? In the back?"

"That pompous jackass was never my boss, and he got it with a knife. Couldn't risk shooting him, and I couldn't let him see it coming. The fool would have yelled his head off and brought down all those redskins on us."

Dan was encouraging him to talk, stalling for time while his mind raced ahead trying to think of something to do.

"Is that what you've got planned for me?" he asked. "A knife in the back?"

The outlaw sneered.

"Since you wanted it face-to-face, I reckon I can oblige you."

Dan shifted his weight in the saddle, every nerve in his body tensed for action.

"So long as I'm not armed, is that it?"

"Shut up!"

The outlaw raised the barrel of the revolver slightly, a signal that he was about to use it. Dan dove from the saddle an instant before Draper fired. He hit the ground hard and rolled into a nearby patch of darkness.

Draper cursed and swung his horse around to trample his enemy. But Dan had never stopped moving, and he was scrambling deeper into the stand of trees where he was protected from the hooves by trunks and branches. He'd left his rifle back in its scabbard, and was armed only with a knife and his fists.

"Give it up and come on out, Newland!" Draper yelled. "I'll make it easier on you."

The outlaw was poised on the edge of the woods, hesitating to enter where he couldn't see, and where it was difficult to maneuver. Dan crouched on his knees, and without making a sound, he crawled back until he could reach out and touch the flank of Draper's mount.

With a lunge, he grabbed the surprised gunman and pulled him from the saddle. As soon as he hit the ground, Draper twisted in an effort to turn the revolver on his attacker, but Dan kicked the outlaw's hand, sending the weapon flying. Draper yelped in pain and faced him. They were clear of the trees, and with Draper unhorsed and weaponless they were even now.

The outlaw landed the next blow, reopening the wound in Dan's side and causing him to gasp. But before Draper could follow up, Dan gave him an uppercut to the jaw that sent him reeling. Draper was furious and he'd lost all reason. He put his head down and charged, aiming to ram his opponent in the gut. Dan sidestepped the assault, and when Draper fell on his face from his own momentum, Dan put his knee in the outlaw's back and pulled his arm up behind him, jerking it tight.

"It's over," he said as Draper lay there making noises that sounded more animal than human.

"Not quite" came a voice from above them.

Chapter Fifteen

Tony stood in the doorway shaking dust from a rag rug. It was a way of taking out her frustration and anxiety, and she shook it with vigor. She looked up to see Aaron riding into the clearing. She could tell that something was wrong by his haste, as well as by the grim expression on his face. Dropping the rug, she ran to meet him.

"Where's Ash?" he asked as he dismounted.

"He was fixing a bridle awhile ago. I think he's still in the barn."

Aaron headed toward it on the run with Tony following only a couple of steps behind him.

"Did you find Dan, and is he all right?" she called.

Concerned with getting to her grandfather, he didn't answer. When he reached the door he shoved it open. She followed him inside. Ash looked up from his work, surprised by Aaron's sudden appearance.

"Slow down there, boy, and catch your breath."

They waited while he did.

168

"Dan sent me with a message," he said after a moment. "He wants Flagg, Allander, and Kearney to come with me to the Circle K. He's gone on ahead to keep an eye on things."

Her grandfather looked skeptical. "You mean he's plannin' on storming the fortress with just the five of you. That's even riskier than trying to sneak into the place alone."

"Well, he was able to get Keaton out of there, all by himself, just before the snowstorm hit. He was taking him to Fort Verde to turn him over to the authorities when Draper caught up with them."

Tony and Ash listened while Aaron related the events that had followed. When he got to the part about the outlaws abandoning Dan to the Apache, she got mad. When he got to the part about the aftermath of the raid on the Timberlake place, she felt sick. She wasn't acquainted with any of those who'd been killed, but it really didn't matter, for they shared a common humanity.

"We can't let Keaton go on running roughshod the way he's been doing," Aaron declared, "for it's just going to get worse, and I think you know that. I promised Dan that I'd fetch the men and meet him near the Circle K."

Ash put the bridle down.

"Then I expect you'd better round 'em up and get moving."

Tony churned with mixed feelings. There was relief and joy that Dan was still alive and, by Aaron's account, in good physical condition. Then there was dismay at what had happened at the large, well-guarded Timberlake ranch. Finally, there was concern about what might happen at the Circle K if it came to a showdown, and it looked like it was going to.

She stood near the house and watched as the four men rode out of the clearing within an hour of Aaron's arrival. She wished fervently to be with them. Her grandfather had been keeping her under his watchful eye, though, as if he could read her thoughts and was afraid that she'd act on them. When Aaron and the others were out of sight, she reluctantly went back to work. Having to stay behind to do nothing more than wonder what was going on was galling to her spirit.

Tony led her mare out of the corral and took her to the barn where she tried to achieve a sense of calmness by brushing her coat. She talked softly to her while she made the coat gleam. Emma pulled the door open and stepped inside.

"So there you are, Tony."

"Where else would I be?" she asked, aware of the surliness in her voice and not really caring. "Certainly not out with Aaron where I could be of some help."

From the corner of her eye, she saw Emma smile.

"Believe it or not, Tony, I can understand your feelings. In your place I'd feel exactly the same way."

Astonished that she would say such a thing, Tony turned and looked her in the eye, again noting the world-weariness in the older woman's features.

"The question is, Emma, what is it that you'd do if you were in my place?"

Emma hesitated before she answered.

"Your grandfather would wring my neck if I told you the truth and he found out about it."

"Tell it anyway," Tony challenged.

"Okay, here it is. I'd saddle a good strong horse, and when nobody was looking I'd take out of here and follow the others. Not to get too close, mind you, but you already know where they're headed, and you know the way. Ash tells me you've done this sort of thing before, so you've got the nerve. Besides that, a reliable firearm, and plenty of ammunition, what else do you need?"

The woman was right. Her grandfather would wring Emma's neck if he knew what advice his houseguest was giving his impulsive granddaughter. But Tony, on the other hand, could kiss her. It didn't take long to make the decision.

"I'll saddle the mare. Grandpa keeps a Winchester and some cartridges in the bunkhouse. I think I can sneak them out of there with nobody being the wiser."

She would be leaving Ash, Emma, and Jacob alone to guard the place, but the Apache would be far away by now, and the rustlers would soon be on the defensive.

"You do love him, don't you?" Emma said. "I'm afraid it shows."

Love was a strong word, but she knew Emma was right. She nodded assent.

"Good. That's a precious feeling, and I think that Dan returns it from the way he looks at you when he thinks you're not watching."

Tony felt reassured, and was grateful. But she was anxious to follow Emma's advice and be on her way.

She threw a saddle on the mare while her new friend watched.

"I'll go to the house now, Tony, and distract your grandfather," she said. "See if you can find that Winchester."

Tony touched her arm. "Thanks for helping me to find my nerve."

Emma smiled.

"Good luck, and bring your young man back safely."

Tony tossed the curry comb onto the bench, and as an afterthought said, "I haven't got around to saying it before, but welcome to the family."

Tears sprang to Emma's eyes, and Tony knew that she'd just given the woman the best gift she could have possibly given.

She waited a few minutes for Emma to get to the house. Then she hurried to the bunkhouse, leading the mare. The Winchester and a box of cartridges were where she remembered them to be.

Tony climbed into the saddle and rode away, taking care to keep the bunkhouse between herself and the house until she was out of sight. When it looked like she'd gotten away, she filled her deprived lungs with air, for she'd been holding her breath. After a quiet thank you to Emma, she concentrated on following the trail that would lead her to Aaron and the other three, and eventually to Dan.

She wondered what she would do if she ever came face-to-face with the man who was responsible for her Uncle Simon's death. No punishment came to her mind that would be sufficiently painful to repay him for what he'd destroyed. Tony recalled the story that Dan had told her shortly after he'd been wounded, the one about civilization beginning in the shadow of a gallows. Since there had always been men around like Keaton and Draper who plundered and killed without a thought for their hapless victims, she was willing to concede that the story had a lot of truth in it, albeit a sad truth.

Tony continued alone in the wilderness until a rumbling in her stomach made her aware that she'd not eaten in hours. She regretted not having been able to bring along something to sustain her, but that would have meant going up to the house and confronting Ash. She'd dared not risk that. At least she'd brought along a canteen of water. No matter about the food, she comforted herself. The others would have plenty of food, and they'd share it with her once she finally caught up with them.

Most of the signs of the snowstorm had disappeared, although it was clear that winter was breathing down on the high plateau country. From time to time, she could hear the rattle of aspen leaves, for much of that gold had turned into the brittle silver ghosts that shook in the breezes. How close she'd come to losing all of this. She was grateful to whoever had ordered that lieutenant's early transfer, for the last thing in the world she wanted was to be stuck in an Eastern boarding school like her mother had attended. Her grandfather meant well, but he failed to understand how much this land meant to her, and how important it was for her to be free of the silly constraints of "polite society."

Since Dan's arrival, she'd begun to think about romance, and even to yearn for it. She'd started imagining herself getting married and raising a family, and she wondered if this part of the country would ever have the peace and stability that would make such things a sensible way of life. Only the future could give her the answer.

It was growing late, and Tony realized that she was going to have to stop soon or else risk getting lost in the darkness. Just a little farther, she promised, for she knew that the men would be stopping and making camp. It was her chance to catch up to them. The trees around her had thinned, letting in enough moonlight to enable her to see, and allowing her to justify going another mile or so.

Tony was making her way carefully along the side of a low ridge, when she heard the sound of a horse whinnying. It brought a sense of relief, for she'd caught up with Aaron and the others at last. Within minutes, she was beside the campfire, among friends, sharing their grub. Her welcome had been qualified, which was no surprise, for they were going into battle. They didn't want her along to look after and worry about, which is what they thought they must do. Nonetheless she'd accomplished her mission. She'd struck out on her own and had taken her place on the front line. The thought brought her a huge feeling of satisfaction.

They broke camp early at Aaron's urging, and soon they were riding toward the Circle K. Just as dawn was showing its colors, they reached the place where Dan was supposed to be waiting for them. He wasn't there.

"Where the dickens is he anyway?" asked Aaron, who was clearly worried.

"Are you sure this is where he told you to meet him?" Allander asked.

"Of course, I'm sure," Aaron replied with a touch of ice in his voice.

Tony knew that they were all worried about the same thing she was. Dan might have been captured or killed.

"I guess that maybe we ought to lie low and watch the place for a spell," advised Kearney.

The rest of them agreed, so they waited silently and watched, hidden from view by the woods—but, as it turned out, not for long, for two of Keaton's men walked out to the corral, saddled their horses, and rode off.

"What do you think about a couple of us going and fetching 'em back here?" Flagg asked. "We might be able to get 'em to tell us something about what's been going on, and at any rate that would be two more coyotes out of the way."

"That's an excellent idea; I'll go with you," Kearney volunteered. "They don't seem to be in any hurry. We can waylay them up yonder, and they won't know what happened. Might not even have to fire a shot."

Tony was skeptical that the capture could be so easy. But they proved her wrong. Kearney and Flagg came back shortly, bringing with them at gunpoint two of the men who'd attacked the ranch under Keaton's orders.

"One of these varmints was telling us that there's only three of 'em left over there," said Flagg, nodding in the direction of the bunkhouse and corral. "He told us that Keaton has turned up dead. Said

that Draper is staying in Keaton's house now, just
like he owned it. He also mentioned that both Draper
and another man named Harvel is gone. They disappeared some time during the night.''

"Then let's pay a visit to the three that's left,''
Aaron said. He pointed to the captured duo. "You
two ride out in front so your pals won't start
shooting.''

"Tony, you stay back here for a little while until
the rest of us see how this is going to go,'' Kearney
ordered.

Reluctantly she watched as the men moved ever
closer to Keaton's compound.

"Hey boys, come on out!'' shouted one of the
prisoners at Flagg's prodding. "Everybody is gone
but us, and these here fellows from the Lazy Q want
to have a talk.''

She saw a flash of red at the window as someone
inside took a quick look. Then it was quiet for a
time while they came to a decision. Soon the door
opened, and one at a time all three emerged with
their hands in the air.

"You boys took part in attacking the Lazy Q and
trying to burn it down,'' Kearney accused, all the
while keeping his rifle pointed at them.

"We was just following orders,'' came the reply.

"Well, a good man was shot down while you was
following them orders,'' Aaron said. "Tie 'em up.''

Tony watched as Flagg and his good-looking partner, Allander, tied the outlaw's hands. Kearney and
Ash kept their rifles handy.

"Let's shut 'em up in the bunkhouse for now,''
Aaron ordered. "We've got other work to do.''

Tony rode up to the little group. Somehow, she didn't feel as much anger for the prisoners as she did for Keaton. With the news of the outlaw's death, she wasn't sure what to do with that anger anymore, although it remained like a hard knot inside her. Then she remembered about Keaton's partner, there was still Draper. . . .

"If we're going after Dan, we'd better get a move on," she urged.

She knew there was reason for concern, for Dan must have seen Draper and the other man sneak out during the night, and had decided to follow them. But following two outlaws alone was a dangerous business.

"They're supposed to have headed north," Aaron said after a few more words with the prisoners. "None of 'em seem to know what they were up to, but it shouldn't be too hard to find their tracks."

It seemed to Tony that time was dragging its feet as they made their way northward in search of the two outlaws and their own foreman. She knew that Dan could handle tough situations. He'd done it more than once since his arrival, and evidently many times before that. But Draper was as dangerous as a rattler, and he apparently had some help in the form of a man named Harvel.

"They've sure come a long way," Allander observed after miles in his saddle without finding them. "Do you suppose they're headed for the mountains?"

"Who knows" was the only answer he got.

Tony too was beginning to wonder just how far

they would have to go, when she caught sight of three horses in the distance.

"Could that be Dan?" she asked hopefully.

"There's only one way to find out," Aaron said. "Let's go."

Chapter Sixteen

At the sound of a stranger's voice, Dan looked up to find himself staring at the business end of a revolver. He raised his hands.

"Harvel!" Draper cried in surprise. He struggled to his feet.

"Stay right where you are," he was ordered. "You didn't expect company, did you, Ben. Thought you could just take over and then sneak off with anything whenever you want. Appears you're not so smart as you think you are."

Harvel was small and wiry, and he wouldn't be a match for either one of them in a fist fight, but he was holding an equalizer. He was one of Keaton's outlaws who'd noticed Draper leave. He must have known about the gold, or at least suspected it.

Harvel stepped over to the sorrel that had belonged to Keaton and that Draper had taken for himself.

"You've got mighty heavy saddlebags," he observed. "I think maybe I'd better have a little look-see."

Both Dan and Draper were on their feet when he reached over and undid one of the saddlebags. The horse was nervous from the fighting that had taken place near his feet, making it it more difficult task.

"Calm down, boy," Harvel said in a soothing voice. "I always did think you was way too good for that slob Keaton to be strutting around on."

Dan heard the clink of metal, and Harvel pulled out a gold piece the size of a double eagle.

"Well, well," he said. "I'm disappointed in you, Ben, for not sharing all of this with the rest of us. Don't you think that would have been the friendly thing to do?"

Draper was clenching and unclenching his fists. For an answer, he snarled.

Harvel was clearly enjoying himself.

"Now, Ben, don't be like that. I could just shoot the both of you right now, head for New Mexico, and nobody would be the wiser. But I propose a partnership instead."

"What kind of partnership?" Draper asked suspiciously.

"Well, a couple of saddlebags full of gold is nice, but I got something bigger in mind, like a sizable piece of the Territory. Ben, you and me could take over the Circle K for ourselves and expand it by annexing all of those two-bit ranches around it one at a time. The men are afraid of you, and they'll do whatever you say. With my brains and your fast gun to back me up, it wouldn't be no trouble at all."

It seemed to Dan that was pretty much what Keaton had in mind before his death, and he could tell that the proposal didn't set well.

"In case you didn't notice, you lamebrain, I'm already running the Circle K," Draper said with a note of arrogance.

"Are you really? It looked to me like you was out here in the middle of nowhere getting your backside beat off."

That was too much for Draper's already wounded pride.

"You worthless saddle tramp!" he yelled as he covered the distance between himself and Harvel in one leap. Dan didn't wait around. He left them to their struggle and headed into the woods.

The sabino had galloped away after Draper's first shot, so Dan was on his own. He ran deeper into the stand of trees, hoping that the conflict would last long enough for him to escape. A branch scratched the side of his face, but he scarcely noticed. Somewhere behind, there was the sound of a gunshot. After that—nothing. Dan knew that one of them would be coming after him.

He paused in the deep shadow of a tree to catch his breath. His wounded side was hurting, and his hand touched blood-soaked cloth. He pulled the bandanna from around his neck and pressed it against the flow. If he tried to run again in the darkness, whichever one was after him would hear the sound. Silence was his ally.

He heard a distant click of hoof on stone. The killer was coming for him. He pulled out his knife, testing its balance in his hand from long habit. Draper was ruthless, even more so than the other, and Dan had a gut feeling that it was he who'd survived. There were all of the old scores to settle, and Dan hoped that it would be the Texan who was left so that he could settle them.

"Newland!" Draper yelled. Dan had gotten his wish.

"Come on out from wherever you're hiding your cowardly carcass, Newland. Let's finish up what we started."

Dan stood still, listening to the horse pick his way through the trees, coming ever closer. Off to the side, there was the sudden movement of a small animal that had been startled from its lair. The rustle of leaves was followed by two quick shots.

Dan didn't move a muscle.

Draper laughed, and the sound was chilling.

"That was just practice, Newland. The next one's for you."

Dan's senses were acute and his nerves were taut. His body and brain had readied themselves for combat.

As Draper drew closer, Dan let his knees slowly bend, bringing him lower until his hand touched the ground. He felt around the area beside him, groping for anything that could be used as a projectile. At last, his fingers closed on a rock that was about a third the size of his hand. Now he was ready. Still he waited. A moment passed, and another. Then he hurled the stone. It landed with a thump, somewhere to the left of Draper, in a growth of underbrush. The outlaw emptied his revolver into what he thought was his enemy.

Dan wasted no time. At the sound of the first shot, he was running toward the outlaw, whose attention was directed toward the underbrush. Gunfire covered the sound of his footfalls. With one hand, he grabbed Draper's arm and pulled him from the horse. With the other, he brought the knife up under Draper's throat.

The outlaw slapped the blade aside with the flat of his left hand, but not before Dan inflicted a deep cut. At the same time, the outlaw kicked hard and threw him off balance. As he struggled to his feet, Dan heard Draper's revolver click on an empty cylinder. Draper tossed it aside and lunged toward the horse for a shotgun. The horse was skittish and side-stepped, causing Draper to miss his chance.

Before the outlaw could try again, Dan grabbed his shoulders and pulled him backward. But he jabbed his elbow hard into Dan's injured side, causing him to double over in pain and release his hold. This time, Draper was able to grab the butt of the shotgun and swung it like a club. Dan saw it coming just in time to avoid a punishing blow. He was dizzy from pain and loss of blood, and no match for his maniacal enemy.

Again Draper swung his club. Dan had no time to think, and no choice. He crouched and lunged, plunging the knife deep into Draper's chest. The outlaw staggered backward, trying to pull the knife from the center of a blossoming stain. Then he fell.

''Newland,'' he gasped, but Dan couldn't hear the rest. Soon it was clear that he never would.

He hoisted the body onto the sorrel that had once belonged to Keaton and led it back through the woods. At the edge of the meadow, he found what was left of Harvel. The man had paid a steep price for his greed, and for the mistake of underestimating Draper.

It was daylight now. He rounded up the sabino and the black that Harvel had ridden. Then he checked the gold-filled saddlebags. Keaton had done pretty well for himself, not that the gold would ever do him or Draper any good.

Dan climbed into the saddle, and with the other horses and their cargo in tow, he headed back the way he'd come. By this time, Aaron would be wondering what had happened to him, and why he wasn't where he said he'd be waiting.

He did some quick subtraction, and figured that there were only five of the outlaws left. Aaron and the other three could take care of the five if need be.

Dan wondered if they'd gotten away from the Lazy Q without Tony this time. Thinking of her and her impulsive ways brought a smile to his face in spite of the pain that was throbbing in his side. She had brightened his life since he'd met her, that was for sure, and he found himself wanting to see her again.

He'd retraced about half the distance, when he caught sight of the riders. There were five of them, and right away, he recognized one of the horses was Tony's mare. They'd seen him, as well, and were coming toward him at a gallop.

"Well, I'll be . . ." Kearney said when they rode up. "You've sure as sin been busy this morning."

"Maybe a little," Dan said, managing a weak smile.

Then Tony and Aaron were gently pulling him out of the saddle. As he lay on the ground, she tore his shirt open and started caring for his wound. The others waited.

He reached up and touched her hair.

"You won't believe this," he said, "but I was more than halfway expecting you to show up at this party."

"Really?" she replied as she gently packed his wound. "I guess you're finally getting to know me, then."

Kearney knelt beside him.

"You don't need to worry about the ones back at Keaton's place. We got 'em. But I wonder how come Draper took himself a new partner."

"He didn't. Harvel followed him, wanting a share. It's a long story and I'll explain it on the way."

"Then come on," Tony said, pulling him to his feet. "Let's go home."

Dan liked the sound of that word. He liked it a lot.